FOOD, GIRLS, AND OTHER THINGS I CAN'T HAVE

A NOVEL BY ALLEN ZADOFF

EGMONT

USA

NEW YORK

EGMONT
We bring stories to life

First published by Egmont USA, 2009
This paperback edition published by Egmont USA, 2011
443 Park Avenue South, Suite 806
New York, NY 10016

10 9 8 7 6 5 4 3 2 1

www.egmontusa.com · www.allenzadoff.com

THE LIBRARY OF CONGRESS HAS CATALOGED THE HARDCOVER EDITION AS FOLLOWS:
Zadoff, Allen.
Food, girls, and other things I can't have / Allen Zadoff.
p. cm.
Summary: Fifteen-year-old Andrew Zansky, the second fattest student
at his high school, joins the varsity football team to get the attention of a
new girl on whom he has a crush.
ISBN 978-1-60684-004-7 (hardcover) — ISBN 978-1-60684-051-1
(reinforced library binding) — ISBN 978-1-60684-194-5 (eBook)
[1. Overweight persons—Fiction. 2. Popularity—Fiction.
3. Self-perception—Fiction. 4. High schools—Fiction.
5. Schools—Fiction. 6. Football—Fiction.] I. Title.
PZ7.Z21Fo 2009
[Fic]—dc22
2009016242

Paperback ISBN 978-1-60684-151-8

FT
Pbk

Printed in the United States of America

CPSIA tracking label information:
Random House Production · 1745 Broadway · New York, NY 10019

For my mother

fat runs in the family.

My name is Andrew Zansky.

I'm fifteen years old, and I weigh 307 pounds.

Actually, I weighed myself yesterday on Mom's digital scale, and I'm down to 306.4.

306.4 is big at my age. Okay, it's big at any age. It's not big enough that they make a Discovery Channel documentary about you, but it's big enough that you stand out wherever you go. There's no flying under the radar at 306.4. There's a lot of surface area to reflect radar signals.

Dad says I carry it well. That means I don't look more than 275. It doesn't make me feel any better.

Mom says being fat is not my fault. She says I have a glandular problem. She says it runs in the family.

Grandma Isabel was fat. So was Papa Joe. Papa Paul is chunky, but I'm not sure how chunky, because he lives in Florida and we hardly ever see him in person. He learned to use e-mail last year and now he sends us photos. He looks pretty big in the photos. He's always wearing a loose shirt, and his skin is very pale. For me, those are important clues. Most people take off their shirts in Florida, and their skin turns brown like car leather. But when you're fat, you don't take off your shirt for any reason. Not for the doctor, not at the beach, not anywhere. That's why I think Papa Paul is bigger than he looks.

Speaking of shirts, I sometimes wear two—my regular shirt and a T-shirt underneath—just in case I'm hit by a car on the way to school. If the paramedics have to cut off my shirt to save my life, there will be another shirt underneath. It's bad enough to get hit by a car. But to be hit by a car and have your blubber hanging off the side of an ambulance stretcher on WBZ-TV? No, thank you.

My mom isn't fat exactly, but she's always fighting her weight. When I say always, I mean all the time. 24/7. It doesn't help that she's a caterer. It's hard to be thin when you're a caterer. She has to taste things, right? Mom's problem is that she doesn't taste a little bit, she tastes the whole thing. Then she complains that her pants are tight and her life is ruined. Then she complains that *my* pants are tight and *my* life will be ruined if I don't go on a diet. It's what they call a never-ending cycle.

There's a lot of fat in our family, but there's some thin, too. Dad is thin and athletic, and my sister Jessica is super skinny. She's also a super bitch, so there's clearly no correlation between being skinny and being nice, at least in her case.

That's my family. Some of us are fat, some are thin.

It may be true that we have a glandular problem, but if so, it's extremely selective.

wake up, get up, suck it up.

I hate my pants. Especially right now. The first day of school.

They're sitting on the dresser taunting me, waiting for me to try them on.

I don't like that they're size 48. I also don't like that they're Levi's, and the company puts the size on the waist where everyone can see it. Are they crazy? Nobody brags about wearing size 48. If Levi's were cool, they'd have a cutoff point at size 32. Even if you bought jeans bigger than that, the waist would still say 32. They could come up with a good marketing slogan for it. "Tease-Proof Pants." Something like that. Then people like me could wear them without having to erase the label for an hour.

Okay, I admit it. I erased the number, but really gently so it looks like it wore out on its own because of my belt, not because some fat kid erased it. Really, what choice did I have? If I walk through school with size 48 on my waist, it's social suicide. I might as well wear one of those yellow-and-black OVERSIZE LOAD stickers they put on trucks.

The pants are sitting next to a preppy button-down, brown-checkered socks, and a pair of blue underwear. Mom laid them out last night before I went to bed. She still picks out my clothes for me. Embarrassing, right? She wants to control everything that goes on my body and everything that goes into it, too. It's because she wants me to be thin. If I can't be thin, she wants me to look thin. And if I can't look thin, she thinks I should act thin.

When Mom looks at me, she sees a fat kid. Which makes her about the same as the rest of the world. They don't see Andrew. They see big.

These are the kinds of things I think about when I'm getting dressed. Crazy, right?

These pants have to fit. They have to, or I can't go to school. No school means no degree, no degree means no college, and no college means I'm pumping gas at a Mobil station in Roxbury. According to Dad, that's the fate of all kids who don't have a 4.0 when they graduate. So I pick up the Levi's, suck in my gut, and pull them up. I'm not even at my waist and I already know I'm in trouble. My pants hate me. They don't want to be seen with me. They want to find a nice size 32 kid and hang out with him.

I grasp at the waist, suck in my stomach, and pull forward and in. The two sides move slowly across the Grand Canyon of my gut, until finally, miraculously, the metal button slips through the slot.

They're on. Barely.

Just once I want to button a pair of jeans and still be able to breathe. It doesn't seem fair that I should have to choose between pants and oxygen.

I glance at the clock.

7:02. In an hour I'll be sitting in homeroom. The thought makes me want to get back into bed and stay there until graduation.

I notice a piece of paper on my night table. It's got my writing on it. I pick it up and take a look.

Remember April, it says.

April. The girl I met yesterday. Not just any girl. The Girl of My Dreams: Asian Edition.

I dreamed about her last night, and I woke up with a tent in my sheets and wrote myself a note. I guess it made sense in the middle of the night, but this morning it just seems cruel.

Why remember a girl you're never going to see again?

Why think about her at all?

reality bites.

Kids are rushing around this morning, chattering away because it's the first day and they're excited. What's it like to be a kid who's excited about school? I try to imagine it. I guess you don't sit up the night before school thinking about girls you'll never meet again or praying that your pants will fit. You think about how much fun it will be to see all your friends and have girls giggle when you talk to them rather than totally ignore you or walk away.

I open my locker. Number 372 on the third floor. I'm a little concerned because I weigh 306.4. What if my locker number is some kind of omen of things to come?

I start thinking about April again, and it makes me kind of sad and happy at the same time. Suddenly a shadow passes by, and I get body-slammed from the back.

"Watch where you're go—" I start to say, and then I see who I'm about to say it to.

Ugo.

Let me tell you about Ugo. Imagine the ugliest creature in the scariest horror movie you've ever seen. That image in your head? It's attractive compared to Ugo. Seriously.

Ugo says, "You're looking good, Zansky. Did you lose an ounce?"

Actually, it's ten ounces. But I don't tell him that.

"I don't want any trouble this year," I say. Ugo and I have been at war since the first week of ninth grade. I don't even know why. I just know that Dad doesn't like it when I have issues at school. It makes him question his legacy.

"We're not going to have any trouble," Ugo says, "as long as you stay in your locker and don't come out."

"Very funny," I say.

But he's not joking. And to prove it, he starts pushing me into my locker. Now it doesn't take a mathematician to figure out that a 306-pound kid is not going to fit into a school locker. But Ugo's never been bothered by little things like facts.

He puts a giant paw on my back and shoves. I probably wouldn't mind getting in the locker if I could close the door behind me and never come out. I'd stay for the whole semester if someone would slide a thin-crust pizza through the slats three times a day. Preferably Papa Gino's with extra pepperoni.

"Cut it out," I say, my voice echoing inside the locker. I sound like such a pussy. Even to myself. Ugo thinks so, too, because he just pushes harder.

"Hey, Andy," someone says in the hallway.

Ugo lets go. I turn around and see my best friend, Eytan,

standing there. I've never been so relieved to seen a skinny person. It's not like Eytan can do anything to stop Ugo. He's outweighed five to one. But there's less likely to be blood-shed with a witness around. Eytan's my personal version of Amnesty International.

"This may sound slightly cliché," Eytan says to Ugo, "but why don't you fight someone your own size?"

"He is my size, Pretzel Rod," Ugo says.

"Then try someone your own IQ. I think there's a mold culture in the Bio lab."

Ugo crunches his fist like he might punch Eytan in the face, but instead he gives me a super hard shove, so my head whacks into the front of the locker. Great. I'll probably have the number 372 imprinted on my forehead for the rest of the day—48 on my waist and 372 on my head. There goes my Sophomores Who Lost Their Virginity Award.

"Son of a bitch," I say, like I've had enough.

I turn around and face Ugo. Actually, I face his sweatshirt. He's a lot taller than me, and he always wears a sweatshirt, even when it's a hundred degrees. From the smell of it, this sweatshirt hasn't been washed since middle school.

"You want to do something about it?" Ugo says to me.

He reaches out slowly, too slowly, and puts an open hand on the front of my chest and pushes. And just like that, he pins me against the locker.

I'd love to shove him back. Grab him by his sweatshirt and whip him into the wall, bash his head a couple times until he starts crying. I get a flash of those sea-lion fights on Animal Planet, two giant bulls roaring and smacking against each other.

But I don't do anything. I don't fight back at all.

That makes him smile. He even laughs a little.

"You're such a wuss," he says.

What can I say? It's true.

So I stare at the ground. I keep staring until he walks away. Then I brush myself off and pretend it didn't happen. Just like always.

"First day follies," Eytan says. "Don't let him get to you."

I rub my sides where the locker almost tore them off.

"No big deal," I say.

But it's not true. When I look into the future, I see an entire year of misery—hiding from Ugo, never going to the bathroom alone, taking corners wide in case he's waiting. It's a very big deal.

I was hoping Ugo forgot about me over the summer, or maybe there would be a new, pudgy freshman for him to torment.

That's pretty sad, right? When you're such a coward you wish someone else would get it instead of you?

on a new level.

Eytan and I are walking downstairs when I suddenly remember I've got a protein bar in my backpack. I'm not supposed to eat it until right before lunch. Jessica taught me that if you eat a protein bar and drink an entire Diet Coke right from the can, you feel really full because your stomach thinks it ate a whole meal. She didn't tell me you swell up like the *Hindenburg* and leak gas out of your butt for thirty minutes. But I guess it takes sacrifice to lose weight. If I have to choose between skinny jeans and air pollution, I'm willing to compromise.

I reach into my backpack, feel the wrapper crinkle seductively in my hand.

"Are you smuggling illegal contraband into school facilities?" Eytan says.

"It's just a protein bar," I say.

"It may look like a protein bar, but how do I know it's not an illegal recording device?"

"What are you talking about?"

"Okay, check it out. I saw this Web site where a guy turns regular items into little cameras, and then he walks around and looks up girls' skirts."

"You're twisted," I say, but I'm kind of laughing. That's why I like Eytan. He can always make you laugh when things are rough and you don't want to.

"Seriously," he says. "You take a protein bar, core out the center, put in one of those spy cams, and *bam!* You're in business."

"What good is a camera in a protein bar?"

He looks at me like I must be dense. "You drop it on the floor when girls walk by," he says, "and it looks up their skirts. Or you kind of hold it in your hand when you're talking to them. You're talking, but your protein bar is looking at their cleavage."

"You're totally obsessed."

"Call it what you want, but this is our year, my friend. You get your 4.0, Estonia wins Model UN, and I become a man. A Hoochie Coochie Man, in the immortal words of Muddy Waters."

Eytan loves blues music. He also loves sex, even though he's never had any. Getting laid is Eytan's life mission, followed by winning Model UN. We came in sixty-third last year, but we were Botswana, and what can you expect when you're Botswana? This year we were assigned Estonia, and for some reason, Eytan thinks we can go all the way. He thinks he can go all the way, too. Last year he got to second base with Sveta, a German exchange student, but no further. Those last two bases are driving him crazy.

Eytan says, "We're sophomores now, right? That means the freshman girls are going to be looking up to us for support and encouragement." He winks at me. "Play your cards right, and you might become a man, too."

"I'm already a man."

Eytan studies my face. "Son of a bitch. Did you get some this summer?"

"No."

"Seriously. You got poon, didn't you?"

"I didn't get poon. But I met somebody."

"Met her where?"

"At a wedding. One of Mom's events, you know?"

Eytan looks at me with amazement. Like he suddenly respects me or something. Not that he didn't before. But on a new level.

"You have a girlfriend!" he says.

"Not exactly."

"I want photographic evidence—cell phone pictures, image capture—"

The bell rings, and the hall fills with a loud *groan*.

"We'd better go," I say.

"You're not getting off that easily. I expect a full report later."

Eytan swings his backpack up on one bony shoulder. Sometimes I think we shouldn't hang around together. You know how big things look bigger when they're next to small things?

Eytan is halfway down the hall when he calls back to me: "What's her name?"

"Who?" I say.

"Your girlfriend."

"April."

My whole body tingles when I say the name. Suddenly I'm back at the wedding yesterday with music playing, surrounded by the smell of Mom's food.

Remember April, the note said.

And I do.

what happened yesterday.

It was Sunday afternoon, and I was in the function hall at Temple Israel, standing in front of a table of 380 mini éclairs. The éclairs were stuffed with cream. I was stuffed into my suit pants.

Another Sunday, another wedding. That's what it's like when your mom's a caterer.

Mom's not just any kind of caterer. She has a specialty: mini food.

She does platters of mini cheeseburgers, mini club sandwiches, mini pizza bagels, mini muffins. She's famous for her Skinny Mini Caesar Salad, which is a whole Caesar salad made on one piece of romaine lettuce so you can pop it into your mouth with your fingers.

Everyone likes small things. Take my sister, for instance. She's got a waist like a stalk of asparagus, and she's very popular.

Small food, small people. Extremely hard to resist.

Anyway, there was a platter of mini club sandwiches sitting on the table in front of me, and they were calling my name.

Andy, they said. *Eat us.*

I looked around to make sure nobody was watching me, and I scooped one up in my fist—

"I saw that," a girl's voice said.

It was an Asian girl, and she was looking right at me. She was about my age, wearing boxy black glasses that made her look like a genius. I glanced down at her cleavage—it was kind of hard to miss with the dress she was wearing—and I realized she was a *beautiful* genius.

Suddenly I got this strange feeling in my chest. I have to be careful with strange feelings because I have asthma. When I have an attack, it usually starts as a tickle in my chest. The next thing you know, there's a giant fist clenched around my lungs and I'm gasping for breath. That's why I keep an inhaler on me at all times.

"What did you see?" I said to the girl, and I reached in my pocket to make sure the inhaler was there. Like Mom says, better safe than sorry.

"I saw you snag a sandwich. You've got nice moves."

"Not true," I said, even though it's obvious that I did it.

"Why do you have to hide it? Why don't you just eat one?"

"My mom made them," I said. "And she'll kill me if I eat her stuff."

"Your mom's the caterer?" She picked up a mini éclair

and popped it in her mouth like it was no big deal, like a person can just eat a whole mini éclair in public, with everyone looking.

"This is delicious," she said. "What's it like to have a mom who's a caterer?"

I glanced down at my stomach. It was hanging over my belt like a muffin top. That kind of answered the question, right?

"Hello," the girl said. "Anybody home?"

"What?" I said, kind of annoyed. Sometimes I get lost in my head so it's hard to keep up my end of the conversation.

"I'm just being friendly," she said. "Don't pop a blood vessel."

"April," an Asian man with graying hair called.

That was the first time I heard her name.

"Coming!" she said.

"Now," the man said. Then he spit out some rapid-fire foreign sentence.

"Is that your dad?" I said. She nodded. "He's pretty tough, huh?"

"Imagine Kim Jong-il as a dentist," she said.

I got a flash of the Korean dictator drilling a molar, and it made me laugh. This girl sounded like one of the Model UN geeks, funny and smart at the same time.

I really liked her. That was my first problem.

She smiled at me, and I noticed her teeth were super white, whiter than any human being's I've seen.

"You have nice teeth," I said, which even I have to admit was a pretty stupid thing to say.

April lowered her voice to a whisper: "I had teeth-whitening."

"You mean like those strips?"

"No. The real thing. With the laser. Just like the actresses get."

"Are you an actress?"

"No."

"Then why did you do that?" I said.

"I used to look . . . different," she said.

"Different how?"

Before she could answer, a stream of angry Korean came flying across the room. Her dad.

"Shoot," April said. "I have to go."

"Wait," I said.

She was a little surprised. So was I. I'd never told a girl to wait before.

"Wait for what?" she said.

I had to say something. I couldn't let her go thinking I was just a fat kid with a caterer mom. I mean, I am a fat kid with a caterer mom, but there's a lot more to me. I don't know why, but I wanted her to understand that. I wanted to tell her there was more to me that she should know.

"I'm a jock," I said, which was a complete lie.

"You are?"

"Seriously," I said. "I'm an athlete."

"That's cool," she said, but it didn't sound like she believed me.

"You know the sumo wrestlers in Japan?" I said.

"I'm Korean," she said. "Everyone assumes all Asian people are Japanese, but we're not. We're a lot of different things."

"I know that," I said, even though I didn't know. "But you've seen the sumo wrestlers, right?"

"Only on TV," she said.

"You know how they look big, but they're really not big? I mean, they *are* big, but they're big in a muscular way. Like they're famous for being big."

"Okay."

"I'm like them."

"You're a sumo wrestler?"

"No. I'm a jock. A big jock."

"You're a big jock?" she said, then she looked across the room. "I really have to go."

She smiled again. It was like looking into car headlights.

I wanted to say something else. I wanted to say a million things, but I just grunted . . .

. . . and April walked away.

the pitiful life of a narrow.

That's what happened yesterday.

So when Eytan asks me, I tell him I have a girlfriend. I even say her name.

But it's all a lie.

I'd never seen April before yesterday, and I'll never see her again. That's what happens when you're a coward. You don't speak up. Even when it's the perfect time. Even if it's the only chance you'll ever get.

"You know my theory," Eytan says. "Hot girls are always named after months, cities, or flowers. You meet a girl named Magnolia or Dallas—guaranteed hotness. And if you name your daughter April, she's going to have a prom date. It's like you've cut fate completely out of the picture."

Eytan gives me a double thumbs-up and disappears into the crowd.

Sophomore year is ten minutes old, and it's already messed

up. Ugo is on the warpath, I lied to my best friend, and my stomach is killing me.

To hell with my diet. I grab the protein bar out of my backpack. I tear off the wrapper and take a huge bite. I hold the backpack in front of my face for camouflage. I don't want people to see me eating. A fat kid chewing with chocolate smeared on his face? That's a bad first impression.

Just as I'm swallowing, a crowd of football jocks walks by. They're laughing, relaxed, slapping each other on the back and grunting like they own the place.

Who am I kidding? They do own the place.

In the center of the group is this one guy, O. Douglas. If we had kings in high school, O. Douglas would be king. He's the quarterback, a senior, and a superstar. That's three out of three. They say he's being recruited by a bunch of colleges, which I guess is really unusual for Newton. I don't follow sports, so I couldn't tell you which colleges or if they mattered.

When I look at O. Douglas, I feel like I'm from another planet or something. He's from Earth, and I'm from some planet where everyone is fat. Elephantania. On Elephantania, I'm normal-sized, and all the skinny people like O. are the equivalent of midgets. We don't call them midgets. That would be insulting. We have some PC name for it like "narrows." I'm normal, and they're narrows, and everyone feels sorry for them. That's how it is on Elephantania. I get all the girls but nobody wants to date the narrows.

As the jocks pass by, O. Douglas looks in my direction for a second, and I get this thrill in my stomach like I saw Brad Pitt or something. Even if you're a guy and you don't like other guys, you kind of want to know Brad Pitt, right? Sheer cool factor.

O. Douglas lifts his hand in a wave, and I'm just starting to wave back when this girl behind me says, "Hey, O.!" in a really desperate voice.

He wasn't waving to me. He was waving to the girl behind me.

the physics of fat.

God has it in for me. Let me tell you how I know.

I am not the fattest.

You might think that would be good news for a kid in high school, but it's not. There is actually something much worse than being the fattest: I am the second fattest.

It's true. I am the second fattest kid in the history of Newton High School. At least if you're the fattest, you have something to brag about. You're the very worst. You're the bottom of the barrel. You are King of the Freaks.

But second fattest? What is that? That's just another fat kid, a sad statistic of America's obesity epidemic. Everyone cares about obesity in general, but nobody gives a crap about the second fattest kid at Newton High. I saw a documentary on the BBC Channel the other night called *The 687-Pound Teenager*. It was about this kid in Britain who is the size of a small mountain range. That's the kind of world we're living in. You have to weigh more than a quarter ton to get any attention. Being second fattest is hardly worth a mention.

Who is the fattest? His last name is Warner. That's God's other little joke. He's Warner and I'm Zansky, and nearly everything in our high school involves alphabetical order. That means the two fatties are always in proximity, orbiting each other like planets in a gravitational tug-of-war. Warner and Zansky. Zansky and Warner.

As I walk into homeroom, I say a silent prayer that Warner has moved away over the summer. But the minute I get through the door, I see him. He's standing in the back of the room, flipping through a Trig textbook and smiling. Warner is always smiling. It's like he's happy to be fat or something. It's insane. Today he's smiling and sweating. Not just a little bit. He's sweating like a rodeo bull.

I stop dead in my tracks. I see why he's sweating.

They changed the desks.

They're not the folding-desk-and-chair combo we had last year. Those were the kind where you can choose to flip up the desk or keep it down, sort of like a tray table on an airplane. These new desks are not like that. They're the ones where the chair has a half desk locked into place on the side. With this kind of chair, you either fit or you don't.

Warner doesn't. At least he's not sure if he does. That's why he's milling around the back of the room. He's acting like he's at a party, relaxed and casual (not that he'd ever be relaxed and casual at a party), but I can tell it's an act. I hate that I know what he's thinking. I hate that I'm thinking the exact same thing.

Will I fit?

This is the Physics of Fat. Where do I fit? Each new situation is a science experiment. Chairs, desks, doorways, amusement park rides, airline and movie theater seats, pants, elevators—they all raise the same question. What mass will fit into what volume of space, and what amount of force will it take to get it there?

Today's experiment: Homeroom.

An empty desk awaits the mountain of Warner, and two seats away, another waits for me. Between the two desks sits Nancy Yee, a Chinese girl built like a plastic drink straw, and Chen Yu, another Chinese girl who outweighs her by eight ounces or so. The poor girls are doomed to spend high school sitting between Warner and me. Even on a normal day, the back row of our homeroom looks like this:

O | | O

It can't be good for Nancy or Chen's reputation, but I have to say it doesn't seem to bother Nancy Yee. She doesn't care that three Yees could fit into a desk that holds half a Zansky and one-third of a Warner. She just sits there drawing in a sketchbook, staring down at the pages through glasses thick enough to focus a spy satellite. She's wearing plaid shorts over purple tights and some kind of vintage green sweater with sparkly purple flowers all over it. My sister watches, like, twenty-seven modeling shows a week. This is a combo that would definitely make her head explode.

"Hi, Andy," Nancy says like she's happy to see me. She flips her hair back, and I see a double streak of acne, both sides of her face breaking out where her greasy hair rubs against it. "Did you have a nice break?" she says.

"It was okay," I say.

"What do you think of the new desks?"

I think Nancy just won the Stupid Question of the Year Award. But I don't say anything. I have to remember that Nancy is oblivious. A girl who has the body mass of a Twinkie can't imagine not fitting into a chair.

"Take your seats, please," Ms. Weston says. She's really dolled up for the first day of class, almost like she's going to a party rather than school. Some guys call her Desperate Doris because she's always trying to look younger. Even worse is that fact that she's the Spanish teacher. There's something sad about a woman without romance teaching a Romance language. It makes me want to cry and eat a paella.

Ms. Weston calls roll. People are starting to look at the fat kids standing in the back of the room.

Goddam Warner. I wish he would sit down or quit school or change his last name. Something. Anything. But no, he only sweats and pretends to read the stupid Trig and shuffles from one elephant hoof to the other.

"Aren't you going to sit down?" Nancy says. I want to kill her, too.

Ms. Weston calls, "Tackenberg, Thomas, Tiburon . . ."

It's now or never.

I suck in my gut, say a quick prayer to the god of physics, and aim my bulk towards the narrow opening between the desk and the chair . . .

Plop.

I'm in.

It takes a little adjusting, a few grunts of effort, and an embarrassing shifting of blubber around my belt—but I fit.

Ms. Weston's at the end of the alphabet, and she calls Warner's name. He answers from a standing position. She looks at him strangely, then looks at the empty desk. She's about to say something, when she decides to move on. I'm kind of relieved for him.

"Zansky," she says.

"Here," I say proudly and from a sitting position.

I fit, and Warner doesn't.

For now.

a revised history of fat and fifteen.

Good news. I'm in AP American History this year. They started a new pilot program where they moved some of the top sophomores into AP a year ahead of time. Me, Eytan, Nancy Yee, and a couple other kids are actually mixed in with juniors and seniors.

Even better news. The AP American History classroom has tables rather than desks. And there's a new teacher, Ms. Hartwell. She's younger than all the other teachers. Someone said she just got out of graduate school. That means she's not giving us the same tired old lesson plans. She has fresh ideas.

"History is subjective," she announces in the second minute of class. "Who can tell me what that means?"

I want to raise my hand. I want Ms. Hartwell's first impression of me to be special. I'm not just some fat sophomore who got accelerated for good grades. I'm an intellectual. I'm going to get a PhD someday, too, but I'm not sure what subject it will be in. I look around, and none of the other sophomores are raising their hands. Everyone's afraid, especially with these older kids around. There's a super high potential for embarrassment.

A senior with wire-rim glasses pops his hand up. I think his name is Eric. "'Subjective' means it's an important subject," he says.

"Not quite," Ms. Hartwell says with a smile on the corner of her lips.

That makes the class laugh, and Eric looks pissed off.

"Anyone else?" she says.

I'm thinking as fast as I can, looking for some way to get into the game, but I'm coming up blank.

"That means it's not objective. It's someone's opinion," a girl says.

The voice sounds familiar. I shift around to see who said it, but there's a big guy in front of her blocking my view.

"How can history be someone's opinion?" Eric says. "I mean, it happened, didn't it?"

"No," the girl in the back says. "It didn't happen."

The class laughs uncomfortably. Whoever she is, she's got serious attitude. Ms. Hartwell raises an eyebrow. I look over at Eytan, and I can see he's excited. He's rubbing his hands together like he's ready for some action. He lives for this stuff.

"That's stupid," another guy says. His name is Justin. I recognize him because he was vice president of Model UN last year, and that's my only club. Eytan's, too. Eytan nominated me for chairman of the Botswana Election Committee, but Justin was a dick and blocked me. He said a freshman didn't have enough experience to be chairman. Then he gave the position to some cute girl.

Now he tries to block the girl in the back. He says, "Things happen, and people write about it, and those things become history, right? That's what history is."

Most teachers would jump in and explain it now, but Ms. Hartwell doesn't say anything. She just folds her arms like we're discussing something really important, and she's got all the time in the world. She shifts her attention back to the girl I can't see.

"Would you care to elaborate, Ms. . . . ?"

"April," the girl says. "April Park."

My heart drops about forty-seven feet and bounces up into my chest. I'm not sure I believe in God, but moments like this get you thinking, you know?

I get a sharp elbow in the ribs. Eytan is staring at me. "April?" he mouths silently.

Crap. I shouldn't have opened my mouth earlier.

Ms. Hartwell says, "What do you think, Ms. Park? Is that a correct definition of history?"

April bites at her lip for a second, thinking hard. She's wearing a pink Izod that reveals a little V of honey-almond skin below her neck. I happen to like honey and almonds. Especially when they're together. She has on those same genius glasses, only now that we're in AP History, they don't seem so out of place.

"I don't think that's an accurate definition," April says. "It reminds me of when we learned about World War Two in my old school."

"What about World War Two?" Justin says with a sneer.

"How did it end?" April says.

"Duh," Justin says. "We won."

"We kicked ass!" Eric says, and the class laughs.

"But the Japanese don't think so," April says. "They think they were on their way to a compromise surrender, and we committed a crime by dropping the bombs."

"Why would we do that?" this Goth girl says.

"The Japanese say we're too arrogant to compromise," April says.

"Ah, yes. History repeats itself," Eytan whispers to me.

Justin rolls his eyes like April's an idiot. "That's not the real story," he says. "That's Japanese revisionism."

"First of all, I'm not Japanese," April says. "I'm giving an alternate view."

"Ladies and gentlemen, we have entered the spin zone," Eric says.

I can see April's pissed.

"It's like my parents," I say all of a sudden.

The attention shifts in my direction. I feel sweat break out under my arms. I glance at April. She looks surprised.

Ms. Hartwell says, "Yes. Mr. . . . ?"

"Zansky."

"Tell us, Mr. Zansky."

Eytan looks at me like I'm nuts. The seniors lick their lips.

"I went to Hyannis Port with my family a few summers ago," I say. "We were walking through town, and my sister got lost. She was, like, seven, and she wandered away from us in the crowd."

Eric makes a loud yawning sound. I want to crawl into a hole and die, but I can't give up so easily with April listening.

"Right away my folks started blaming each other," I say. "Mom said it's Dad's fault Jessica got lost because he wasn't paying attention. Dad said it's Mom's fault because she was supposed to hold her hand. But probably it was nobody's fault. I mean, Jess is a kid and she got distracted, right? But they were so freaked out they just yelled at each other and bolted in different directions. So I stopped and I tried to think like Jess. Where would she go? What does she like? And I looked behind us and I saw these shirts hanging in a doorway that have all kinds of animals on them, like cutesy Asian stuff."

I shouldn't have said "cutesy Asian stuff." Maybe that's an insult to April. Maybe now she thinks I'm a jerk. I glance at Nancy Yee for a status check, but she's sketching in a little book.

"What happened then?" Ms. Hartwell says.

"I pulled my parents into the store, and we found Jessica."

"News flash. You're from a dysfunctional family," the Goth girl says.

Half the class cracks up.

"What's your point?" Justin says.

I don't know what my point is. I don't know why I told this story. I glance at the clock, hoping lunch is coming soon.

"Well?" April says. She sounds kind of snooty, and I hate her for it.

I take a deep breath. Focus.

"I guess my point is that Jessica got lost, and right away my parents started making up stories about it. Nobody bothered to find out what really happened. They couldn't even see the truth. That's what history really is. It's people making up stories to suit themselves. Different countries, different parties, different stories."

"Whoa," Eytan says. "That's deep."

Ms. Hartwell nods. "How do they tell the story now, Mr. Zansky?"

"They don't," I say. "They split up."

Everyone's quiet for a second, and then Justin rubs his fist on his eyes. "Waaah," he says like he's a baby crying. The class giggles uncomfortably.

"Screw you," I say really loudly. I feel good about saying it. At least until Justin stands up and cracks his neck like a weightlifter. Come to think of it, Justin is a weightlifter.

"You want to repeat that?" Justin says.

I glance towards Ms. Hartwell, and her eyes are jumping

around like she doesn't know what to do. She might have ideas, but she's never had real students to teach them to. Real students are trouble, and I can see she doesn't know how to handle it.

Justin stares at me, his palms out by his sides. "What's up, bro? You got something to say to me?"

The class is really quiet.

I know I'm supposed to do something, say something, take him on in some way. But I can't. I'm totally frozen. I try to meet April's eye, but she won't look at me now. She just stares at her desk.

That's when Ms. Hartwell pulls it together. "All right. That's enough," she says.

Justin sits down, but he takes his time doing it, sinking slowly. Just before his ass hits the seat, he coughs and says, "Fag" under his breath. A couple guys laugh.

"Let's get back to work," Ms. Hartwell says.

"That guy is ass lint," Eytan whispers to me. "Don't let it faze you."

"It doesn't," I say. I want to be a guy who doesn't give a crap. I want to be a guy who doesn't get fazed.

I want to be a lot of things, but I'm not.

eytan meets the new girl.

Eytan and I walk out of class together. As soon as we're clear, he pulls me aside.

"Is that the April you were telling me about?" he says.

Before I can answer, April walks out of class alone.

"Give me two seconds," I tell him, and I peel away. I have to do something before I chicken out again.

"Hey," I say to April. Not what you'd call a brilliant opening line.

"Hey," she says, but she doesn't sound happy about it. It's not like yesterday when she was teasing me. Maybe I look better with a table of éclairs behind me.

"Remember me?" I say.

"The big jock, right?"

"Yeah." I smile. She doesn't smile, but at least she remembers. I glance over my shoulder at Eytan. He's watching me with a curious look on his face. I don't think he's ever seen me talking to a girl except maybe Nancy Yee. But she's not really a girl. More of a stick figure with an accent.

"Do you go here?" I say to April.

"Now I do," she says. "My dad got transferred over the summer."

"Interesting," I say.

I can feel my heart beating in my chest. The last time I went to the doctor, he had to press the stethoscope into me really hard because he couldn't hear well through my fat. But my heart's banging away so hard right now, it feels like I don't have any fat at all. It's tapping right against the front of my chest. What if I die of a heart attack in front of April? What if her last memory of me is 306.4 lbs. pounds of blubber collapsing at her feet like a dead walrus?

Eytan's slides in next to me. "Eytan Michaeli," he says, and extends his hand.

"I'm April," she says, and they shake.

"I've heard a lot about you from Dr. Zansky here," Eytan says, and he puts his arm around my shoulders. April looks at both of us like we're maniacs. I know Eytan's trying to help me, but he's making it worse.

"April's a new student," I tell him.

"You fell down the rabbit hole, huh?" he says.

"If you have questions about anything . . . ," I say.

"It would be our pleasure to assist you in navigating the madness," Eytan says.

We stand there for a second, Eytan and me on one side, April on the other. People are looking at us with the new girl, and I can see it's making April uncomfortable. You have to be careful who you stand next to when you're new. Eytan and I are not exactly status builders.

"I have to get to class, guys," April says.

"Absolutely," I say. "You don't want to make a bad first impression."

April kind of shrugs like she doesn't need my advice. Then she takes off.

"That was your girlfriend?" Eytan says when she's gone.

"Sort of. I'm hoping. You know."

"Okay, here's my assessment," Eytan says. "First of all, I'm putting aside the fact that you lied to your best friend."

"I didn't lie exactly."

"Your shwanz is making up stories. It's normal. Hormone-induced psychosis."

"I admit I stretched the truth."

"So here's the thing," Eytan says. "Normally, she'd be way out of your league. No offense."

"None taken," I say. He's right about April being out of my league. I know it.

"But seeing as how she's new . . . you might have a chance. You just have to act fast. That's how I got in with Sveta last year. What chance did I have with a hot German exchange student, right? So I moved at the speed of light. *Blitzkrieg*, baby. I had to impress the hell out of her before she had any-one to compare me to."

"You think that will work for me?" I say.

"Only if you dazzle her," he says.

I bite my thumbnail. I'm starting to feel hungry again.

"Fast," Eytan says.

long-distance dad.

"Do you believe in love at first sight?" I ask Dad.

I'm hiding in my bedroom on the cell while Mom watches TV in the living room downstairs. She hates it when I talk to Dad, especially if she's not around to monitor the call.

"Love at first sight," Dad says. "You mean like in a fairy tale?"

"In the real world."

I look down at the iPhone Dad gave me for my birthday. His picture is staring out at me. For some reason, he doesn't quite fit in the frame. His forehead is chopped off. I'm trying to remember the last time I saw him in person. I'm pretty sure he had a forehead, but it's been a while.

"I met this girl," I say.

Dad interrupts me. "I don't want to talk about this, Andy. We have bigger fish to fry."

Dad likes to get down to business. It's because he's a lawyer, and lawyers bill by the hour. Dad's life is measured in billable hours, six minutes at a time. Ergo:

a six-minute phone call to Andrew = $35

a fight with Mom = $140

going to the bathroom (#1) = $5.83

going to the bathroom (#2) while reading *The New Yorker* =$70

messy divorce = $1.4 million

I understand how billable hours gives a different perspective to everything. Time is money after all.

Anyway, I know what fish Dad's talking about. School.

Now that sophomore year has started, Dad's worried. Not half as worried as I am. I'm the one who had to live through ninth grade.

Dad interrupts me. "It's a whole new year," he says, "which makes it like a new start. You know what I mean?"

"I know."

I had a few hundred issues my freshman year, and Dad's concerned I'm going to have a few hundred more this year.

"You're starting behind the eight ball," Dad says. "They've already had a good long look at you. A whole year's worth of impressions. That means you have to overcome before you can triumph."

"That's exactly my plan," I say.

Dad doesn't say a word. The line is totally clear, not a crack or a pop. Just three dollars' worth of silence. When Dad and I stop talking, it feels scary, like looking into a canyon from the very edge.

"What's it like in New York?" I say to try and change the subject.

Dad's been commuting back and forth, making the transition to the new office.

"It's an amazing city. Really something special. Like Boston times three, if you can imagine that."

"Maybe I can go down there with you one time."

"What do you mean?" Dad says.

"Before you move. Just so I know what it's like."

"To tell you the truth, I'm still getting settled," Dad says. "But once things calm down a bit, we'll make a plan."

"I could come one weekend, maybe. I'll take the train so it will be cheaper."

Mom walks by my bedroom door. "Who are you talking to, honey?"

"My friend," I say. Mom usually checks the cell bill at the end of the month and scans it for Dad's number. That's the downside of a family plan. Surveillance. The upside is that she won't know I lied to her for twenty-four days.

"I have to go," I tell Dad.

"Good boy. Don't upset the apple cart."

I click off, and Mom looks at me suspiciously. "Did you do your homework?"

"We've only had one day of school, Mom."

"Well, don't scream at me. I'm your mother, and I want you to go to college."

"I'm so not having this conversation," I say.

this theory I have in the middle of the night.

I'm standing in Coolidge Corner on a winter afternoon. It's really cold out, and I have to blow on my hands and slap them together to keep warm. I try to pull my jacket closed, but it's a size too small and the sides won't meet.

Suddenly I hear brakes squeal as the T stops two blocks away.

April gets off.

She's wearing a red coat, and even from far away I can tell she looks really beautiful. It takes her a minute to see me, but when she does, a big smile crosses her face, and she starts to run towards me. . . .

That's when I wake up.

Crap. It was one of those dreams that you don't know is a dream until after it's over.

My whole body is hot and tingling. It feels like April was right here with me. I can even smell her in the bed next to me. That's totally crazy because I've never been in bed with a woman, and I barely know what April smells like in the first place. Something fruity. That's all I remember.

That's when a theory pops into my head. It's a theory about love at first sight.

I don't know if I believe in love at first sight. It's kind of fairy-tale stuff. But then I start to think, what if love at first sight is the wrong name for it? What's if it's really love at *second* sight? Maybe you fall for someone in one life, and then you don't see them for a thousand years or whatever. Your heart totally forgets about them. Then you meet again, and it remembers.

Maybe that's what happened to April and me. We met a long time ago, and when I saw her at the wedding, I didn't know her, but my heart remembered her.

The problem is her heart didn't remember me.

Okay, theory number two.

Maybe when we met the first time, I was thin—really thin, like a guy who wears size 29 jeans. Or a size 29 toga or whatever. That's why April's heart couldn't recognize me now. It was thinking about the thin guy from the past, and that didn't match the guy standing in front of her.

So she saw me, and maybe she had a little déjà vu, but it wasn't nearly enough.

She needed more time to get to know me. Her heart needed more time.

That's the thing about being fat. People can't see the real you, so you have to work really hard to show them.

Now I've got a second chance, but I have to work fast. Like Eytan said. Super fast.

Love at second sight. I can't tell if this is some brilliant idea, or just one of those thoughts you have in the middle of the night that seems ridiculous when you wake up. Dad used to say you shouldn't trust yourself after two beers or after midnight. I've never had a beer, but I look at the clock and see it's 2:30 a.m., way after midnight.

I write myself a little note and put it on my night table. *Remember love at second sight*, it says.

I close my eyes and try not to think about April. Eventually I fall asleep. Maybe I dream of her, but if I do, I don't remember.

a bad bounce.

I'm not sure I believe in God, but there are times when I could really use him. Right now for instance. Gym class.

We have to wear shorts in gym. It's mandatory. And because the weather is still nice, Coach Bryson has us outside on the soccer field. That means I'm standing in bright sunlight with my elephant legs exposed. I wouldn't mind wearing shorts if I went to a school for the blind. I'd feel very comfortable there. But in the middle of the day surrounded by thin guys with 20/20 vision and the girls about to show up any minute?

This is where I could really use God. I know he can't make me instantly thin or strike the entire sophomore class blind, but I need one small favor from him.

I need him to put April in a different gym class.

Is that too much to ask? Just put April in a different gym class so she doesn't see me running in shorts. Then when she thinks about me, she can think about my brain rather than my blubber.

Coach Bryson surveys the field with his hands on his hips and a whistle clenched between his teeth. He's got a big chest and a thick moustache like a seventies porn star. Some of the guys call him Magnum P.I. He blows the whistle and shouts, "Let's warm up, gentlemen. I don't want any of you superstars tearing a crotch muscle."

He unleashes a bag of twenty soccer balls into the middle of the crowd, and the guys leap on them and start doing all kinds of bounces and trick shots. I only have one trick shot. Pretending I'm sick. Last year I forged a note from Mom to get out of the gymnastics rotation. But I spent a week having panic attacks, thinking I was going to get caught, so I never did it again.

"Let's do a couple laps to get the blood flowing," Coach says. He pats his stomach. "I'd better join you. I've been eating pizza like they just invented cheese."

Coach starts to run, and the guys follow him in a big circle, kicking the balls in front of them. My body is not really built to run. When it runs, it bounces, and when it bounces, things tend to get displaced. Like my shorts. I have to pull up my shorts every twelve seconds, or they'll end up in the grass.

But the guys are running, and I have to at least make an effort. Even though it's gym, you still get a grade, and I'd hate to blow my 4.0 because I'm fat. That seems totally unfair.

There is a bit of good news. Warner isn't here bouncing around next to me. I saw him downstairs in the locker room a few minutes ago coming out of Coach's office. I don't know what he could possibly be talking to Coach about, but whatever it was, he's not up here. That much is a relief.

I do my best to keep pace with the other guys. I pull up my shorts with one hand and wipe my sweat with the other. All the time I'm praying: *Just keep April out of this class, God. That's all I ask for today. You can have Ugo beat the crap out of me, or Mom catch me with a mouthful of mini whatever, as long as you keep April away for an hour.*

"Check it out," one of the guys says, and he points back towards the school.

The girls run onto the field.

It takes about fifteen seconds before I see April come out.

God went on vacation my first week of school. There's no other explanation.

Here's the bright side. April looks good in gym clothes. Really good. She's got on black Adidas shorts with white stripes down the side. When she turns, I can see the outline of her bra through her T-shirt. It takes my breath away, and I didn't have much breath to start with.

April glances in my direction, and without thinking, I speed up. It makes no sense for a guy who can barely run to run even faster, but my body does it automatically. It's like it doesn't give a crap what it can and can't do. When it sees April, it tosses out the rules and starts hauling ass.

Suddenly I'm running super fast, lifting my legs higher than I ever have before. For some reason I think of a horse, one of those royal stallions in England decked out with all kinds of bells and ribbons. The kind that the guys with big fuzzy hats ride, you know? I'm prancing like I'm one of those horses, zigzagging back and forth, doing moves I don't even know how to do.

I'm not the only one. Even Coach sucks in his stomach when the girls' coach comes out. The guys on the field start to get really aggressive once the girls are watching. First they take shots on goal, then a game spontaneously breaks out. I don't know what team I'm on, but I start to play. I fall in with some guys I've never met who are driving towards the goal. A couple guys are shouting, "Pass!" and someone else is screaming, "Over here!" at the top of his lungs.

Somehow I end up in the center of this group, and the goal is suddenly twenty feet in front of me with a super tall kid blocking it. Out of nowhere the ball appears in front of me, right at my feet, and people are screaming at me, "Shoot! *Shoot!*"

It all happens really fast. It's like my brain has switched into some kind of athlete mode I didn't know I had. I can see what I want my body to do—push off from my left leg and kick the hell out of the ball with my right—and I can see where the ball is supposed to go, even imagine one of those *Bend It Like Beckham* thingies where it flies into the air, then arcs left and goes past the goalie.

I imagine the reaction as the guys crowd around me and congratulate me for scoring. The girls on the sideline say, "Who is that guy?" And April says, "I know who he is. That's Andrew Zansky. His mom's an incredible caterer."

It's all a great fantasy, but when the moment comes to kick the ball, my body isn't in the right place. By the time I remember that I've never done this before, and maybe I'm pushing my luck, it's too late. I've committed to some kind of thing that's way, way beyond me.

As soon as I kick, my legs go out from under me. The ball stays where it is, and I go airborne. First I crash into a group of guys. They go down like bowling pins, four or five of them at one time.

But I've got so much momentum that it doesn't stop me. Newton's First Law. An object in motion tends to stay in motion. Especially a fat object.

My entire body flies into the goal. The tall goalie kid screams as I slam into him at, like, a hundred miles per hour.

Even he's not big enough to stop me. That's when I hit the net. For a second I think I'm going to rip through and go tumbling right out into the parking lot. . . .

But the net holds. At least briefly.

It snags me, and then the entire thing comes crashing down on top of me. I see flashes of white nylon and grass and goalpost, and then everything stops. I end up splattered on the grass, tangled so deeply in the net that I can't move my arms or legs.

I look back at a field full of amazed students. It's like a scene from a war movie, bodies splayed everywhere, girls screaming. Coach Bryson is running and blowing his whistle, trying to calm people down. The girls' coach runs inside the athletic shack and appears with a first-aid kit to treat the wounded.

I look around for April. She's standing on the sideline with this horrified expression on her face. She's staring at something, but it's not me. It's in the center of the field.

I follow her gaze until I see what she's looking at. There's something in the grass. A blue-and-white pair of shorts. My shorts.

I feel wind blowing on my legs. I shift around until I can see what's going on.

I'm in my underwear. Not even cool underwear. Fruit of the Loom. White. Size XXXL.

It takes the coaches nearly twenty-five minutes to get me out of the net. They spend the first ten trying to untangle me, and the last fifteen cutting me out with a utility knife they get from the Vocational-Ed teacher.

Most of that time I look up at the sky pretending I'm somewhere else. I'm definitely not tangled in a net in my underwear with forty-nine sophomores watching me. I'm not practically naked in front of the girl I want to impress most in the world.

Coach sends everyone to play a game on the adjacent field, but I can hear them whispering about me and laughing. Just once I look over and see April looking back at me. Our eyes meet, and she turns away like she doesn't know me. I can't really blame her.

I hear the whole story later from Coach. It turns out that when I went to kick, my shorts fell off, and I tripped and took six guys down with me. Four of them got treated in the nurse's office and released, one needed three stitches at the hospital because my elbow hit his chin, and the last one was able to limp off the field under his own power. I'm the only one who wasn't hurt. Coach said it's because my fat protected me like an airbag in a car crash.

"Congratulations," he said, "you've earned a five-star safety rating."

roar.

It takes about five seconds for everyone in school to hear about the soccer game. There's no way to keep secrets in high school, especially secrets involving underpants and personal mortification.

At first people call me Tighty Whitey, Fat Ass, or the Destroyer. But none of those really catch on. Then, a few days later in History class, Justin calls me Jurassic Pork.

That catches on pretty fast.

Now instead of just being some unknown fat kid, I'm JP, Jurassic Pork, the fat dinosaur who steps on people and crushes them.

It's pretty bad for me, but it's worse for Warner. He didn't do anything, but he's guilty by association. Associated fatness or something like that. When people see us together, they make roaring noises. They scream and pretend they're terrified. They say stuff like, "So simple, even a caveman can do it," and they mime throwing spears at us.

Eytan tells me to ignore it, and it will pass. "Immature kids being immature." That's what he says. But it's tough to ignore people taping Brontosaurus pictures to your locker.

That thing Dad said about first impressions? He was right. It's completely possible to change people's first impression of you.

You can make it worse.

the four words she says.

A couple days later I'm on the way to English class when I run into April in the hall. We've been avoiding each other since the soccer game. At least I've been avoiding her. But there's hardly anyone else in the hall now, so we either have to say something or pretend not to know each other.

I slow down a little, and April does, too. I feel that strange sensation in my chest again. It's crazy, but I'm suddenly hopeful. I think maybe the underwear incident wasn't such a big deal. Maybe April is so amazing, she can look right past that kind of thing. She's too smart to care about what people think. I wonder why I've been avoiding her if I could have been talking to her all along.

"How's it going?" I say, and throw her a big smile.

"You told me you were a jock," April says.

My smile goes away. April sounds angry. More than angry. Disappointed.

"What do you mean?" I say.

"At the wedding. You told me you played sports."

"I guess," I say.

"You don't guess. It's what you said."

"Okay, fine. I said it. Why are you so pissed?"

"You lied to me," April says.

Those four words—the way she says them—I swear to God I gain a hundred pounds in a minute. It's not even fat weight. It's heavier than fat. It's something dense and awful, like my blood turns to lead.

"I don't care if you're a jock or not," April says. "That's not what I'm about."

"What are you about?"

She looks at me coldly. "I guess you'll never find out, because I can't trust you."

I suddenly get it. April's not angry that I almost destroyed an entire soccer team, or even that I wear briefs instead of boxers.

She's angry that I lied to her. Which means she was hoping I was the real thing. Which means Eytan might have been right. I really did have a shot. Did. Past tense.

I remember the time last year when Mom and Dad were fighting. It was the day Mom found out about Dad's affair. I think she'd suspected it for a long time, but whenever she asked Dad, he said there was nothing going on. "Nothing to worry about." That's what he always said.

I guess when someone you love lies to you, you want to believe them. At least until you can't believe them anymore. When Dad's sexy paralegal, Miriam, showed up at the house one afternoon to tell Mom what was going on, everything went to hell. Mom started baking mini pecan pies, and she didn't stop until Dad packed his bags and moved out.

April's looking at me like she wants to bake some mini pies, too. She might even grind me up and use me for the filling. Her arms are crossed while she waits for me to say something.

It's really confusing. Some girls are impressed if you lie to try and get their attention. I've seen guys bragging about all kinds of crap, and girls know what's up, but they still fall for it.

It's different with April. It's like I broke her bottom line or something. I broke it, and there's no way to unbreak it.

But I have to try.

I have to tell her about the real me, why I lied that day, all the things I wanted to say to her at the wedding. I want to tell her about the night when I couldn't sleep, and I had those crazy ideas about us at three in the morning.

I want to tell her all of that and more, but when I open my mouth to speak, nothing comes out. That's what it's like to be me. Everything goes into my mouth, but when I need something to come out, I'm out of luck.

I guess April gets tired of waiting, because she spins around before I can say anything and walks away. I stand there, so heavy I can't move, listening to the squeak of her sneakers on the hall floor. I've known April for less than a week, and I've seen more of her back than I have of her front.

That's not how I planned it. Not at all.

the scent of popular.

Things happen really fast after that.

On Monday I'm standing in the hall outside the boys' locker room. The bell has already rung, but I'm afraid to go in. Since the soccer game, I'm not exactly Mr. Popularity in gym class.

Coach passes by on his way into the locker room. "Oh, good," he says when he sees me. "I need to talk to you."

We go into the locker room together, and the guys look at me like I'm dead meat. If Coach wasn't there, I probably would be.

"Let's go into my office," Coach says, and he closes the door behind us.

I've never been in Coach's office before. There are inspirational posters all over the walls. One shows a big chunk of coal like you'd use in your grill. The poster says, *A diamond is a lump of coal that stuck with it.*

"I have good news," Coach says. "I'm taking you out of this class."

For a second I think I won't have to take gym anymore.

"I could have a study period or something," I say.

"No, no," Coach says. "Phys Ed is mandatory. I'm putting you in Modified Gym."

"Mod Gym?" I say. Mod Gym is the class for retarded kids and the handicapped. Everyone calls it Slow Gym. "I can't go into Mod."

"It's for your own safety. And anyway, I think it will be more your speed."

My speed. Slow.

What do you do in Slow Gym? It's more like what you don't do. You don't go outside and play sports with the normal kids. You sit in a circle and roll a kickball back and forth in the gym. No kidding. One hour of rolling a ball. Coach pops in every twenty minutes to make sure nobody fell out of their wheelchair.

If that wasn't bad enough, guess who's in Slow Gym?

Warner.

He's sitting on the ground smiling and spinning a dodgeball between his legs. So we're together yet again.

That's just Monday. Trust me, it gets worse.

On Tuesday, Eytan and I are walking out of AP History when I see Justin put his arm around April's shoulders like he's hot shit. She shrugs it off, but not too fast. It looks like she's grateful to have someone paying attention to her. Someone with a positive rep. Someone who's not me.

Eytan sees it, too, but he doesn't say anything. He starts talking about Estonia instead, trying to distract me like a friend does when things are bad.

At dinner on Tuesday night I have to listen to Jessica telling Mom how things are going so well at school. She loves seventh grade, she says, and then she launches into some stupid story about how the boys try to touch her hair, but she screams and they run away.

Mom asks me how things are going, and I tell her the girls try to touch my hair, but I scream and they run away. Jessica doesn't find that funny, and neither does Mom. So I make up a bunch of exciting stuff, so Mom won't get worried or e-mail Dad to have a talk with me.

So much for Tuesday.

On Wednesday, April's not sitting alone at the new-girl table in the cafeteria anymore. Instead she's at a table with Lisa Jacobs and a bunch of the popular girls. Lisa Jacobs is an SHG. Super Hot Girl, only she's SHG #1. She's got long blonde hair, an amazing face, and giant boobs. Her boobs are so big they're like an entire other student. Eytan says they have their own GPA, like Lisa has a 2.8, and her boobs have a 4.0.

The worst part is that Lisa is nice. Not nice to me, but a nice person. Everyone says so.

What I can't figure out is how April ended up with Lisa. They're laughing together like old friends. When did they become friends?

Lisa is also O. Douglas's girlfriend. No surprise that the hottest girl and hottest guy are together. My dad always says, "Water seeks its own level." Maybe that's why I always get stuck with Warner. Fat drifts towards other fat. It's a fundamental physical law.

Later that day I see April and Lisa Jacobs together again, this time sitting in the library. It looks like they're studying together, but that seems pretty much impossible. I mean, April is brilliant, and Lisa Jacobs is . . . known for having good hair. It's a mystery to me.

On Thursday, I see April walking down the hall with those same girls. They're like a posse now, moving together in a clump of popularity.

By Friday, she's sitting far away from Justin in History class. She's getting so popular, she doesn't need him anymore. Or maybe her new friends warned her that he was a dipshit. Either way, she's moved on to bigger and better things.

That would be kind of a relief, except she's moved on from me, too. She hasn't said a word to me since that day in the hall, and she won't make eye contact. It's like we've never even met. Or maybe we did meet, but she purposely did an *Eternal Sunshine* and had the memory erased to make space for more pleasant memories that don't include fat kids.

Eytan said I had to move fast, and I did.

It took just one week for April, a brand-new girl, to become popular. It took me less than a week to become an untouchable.

That's pretty fast.

mini memories.

I'm standing in front of 175 mini spring rolls with a love song playing in the background. "True Colors," that old song by Cyndi Lauper. Sappy. But what else do you expect at a wedding?

It's the weekend, and I'm helping Mom again. There are girls all over the place, but I can't stop thinking about April. I blame the spring rolls. They're Asian, and so is April. I know she's Korean and spring rolls are Vietnamese, but it doesn't matter. Asian things remind me of April now.

Mom passes me with a platter of mini knishes, and those remind me of April, too. I can't figure that one out. Why would Jewish food remind me of her?

When I see the mini meatballs, I realize it's not the nationality at all—it's the food. Food in general reminds me of April. So I'm pretty much screwed.

As soon as Mom disappears into the kitchen, I stuff three

spring rolls into my mouth. I gulp down a knish and nearly burn the roof off my mouth. Then I pop in a meatball to wash it all down.

True colors.

I'm trying to distract myself, but it doesn't work. I keep looking behind me thinking April is going to walk up at any minute.

And the thing is, she's not even at this wedding.

I turn right.

It's the end of the day, and I'm rushing to put books in my locker and get down to the auditorium for the first Model UN meeting. Eytan has been talking about it nonstop for two weeks. "Are you excited?" he asked me yesterday for the three-thousandth time.

"Absolutely," I said. "But aren't you a little worried about being Estonia?"

That was my subtle way of reminding him that nobody gives a crap about Estonia, and maybe he shouldn't get his hopes up.

"That's the great thing," Eytan said. "We're the underdog. Nobody expects the underdog to do well. It's perfect."

I don't see how it's perfect. I see another long year toiling in obscurity, arguing about sheep-grazing rights with Latvia. When I told Eytan I was excited, I was lying. I just didn't want to hurt his feelings. Now I have to go down to Model UN and fake it for two hours.

I slam my locker closed and spin the dial twice. I turn around and run right into Ugo's sweatshirt.

"People call you JP now. That's funny," Ugo says.

I look up and down the hallway. Nobody. Why is it you can't get two seconds alone all day in high school, but when you actually need people, there's nobody around?

"Jurassic Pork," he says, trying to get a reaction out of me.

"I'm not scared of you," I say.

It's a total lie, and he knows it. He cracks his knuckles.

It's go time.

Suddenly I think about Dad. If I get into it with Ugo, Dad's going to be pissed. Ugo and I had a fight last year, and Dad had to come in for a thirty-six-minute conference. That's $210 in Dad's world. If you add drive time back and forth from work, one stupid fight cost Dad $455. I know the exact number because he wrote me up a fake bill to teach me a lesson.

Now I'm thinking it's going to happen again, only Mom will have to deal with it alone, and she'll freak out. Dad will have to spend seventy-six minutes on the phone talking her down, and forty minutes yelling at me for making his life difficult. I don't want to see what that bill looks like.

So when Ugo makes his move, I do something different. I run.

It's total wuss behavior. I won't deny it. It's not only wuss, it's just plain stupid because I'm fat, and I can't run. They don't put you in Slow Gym because you set records in the hundred-meter dash.

But I'm not thinking clearly in the moment. I'm running for my life.

I'm barely halfway down the hall before Ugo snags me by the back of the shirt and reels me in like a whale on a harpoon. He jerks me around and sends me flying over his thigh. It's like I weigh nothing at all. That's how strong he is.

Once I'm on the ground, he starts kicking me in the ass. "Holy shit," he says, "you're so fat my foot almost disappeared!"

I wish I had super ass cheeks. I'd grab his foot and tear it off with my ass. That would teach him a lesson. But I don't have a super ass or super anything else. I have protective fat and the good sense to cover my balls. That's about it.

Ugo leans back on one foot, getting ready to kick me again. I close my eyes and nothing happens.

I open my eyes and he's not there anymore. I roll over just in time to see him traveling backwards, pulled by some invisible gravitational force. I don't know what's going on until I notice there's an arm pinned around his neck. Someone is pulling him from behind.

O. Douglas is pulling him.

He spins Ugo around, unwinding him like a top until they're face-to-face. It's an expert move, like something you'd see on WWF.

"What the hell?" Ugo says.

"Back off the kid," O. says.

"What's it to you?" Ugo says.

He waits for an answer.

I wait, too, because I've got no idea. I've never even met O. Douglas before. He's got no reason to save me. He doesn't give a reason. He just holds his hands out to Ugo, palms open, and shrugs. Ugo looks at me over his shoulder. He's like a lion who can't get to his meat. I'm practically pooping my pants, but O. doesn't flinch.

"Take off," O. says quietly.

"Whatever," Ugo says, and he drifts away down the hall.

I've never seen anyone stand up to Ugo. This is one of those historic moments in the history of high school. I wish I had it on video so I could play it back for Eytan. He'd upload it to YouTube, see if we'd get e-mail from some lonely girls in the Midwest.

But it doesn't seem to be a big deal to O. Almost like business as usual.

"You okay?" he says.

"I guess."

He holds out a hand to help me up, but I don't take it. I don't want him to think I'm some little kid who can't stand up on his own. I get up by myself and brush dirt off my pants.

O. says, "The bigger they are, right?"

I don't know if that's right or not. Do the laws of physics apply to Ugo? Or is he some kind of anomaly? A giant, sweatshirted version of a black hole.

O. motions towards the stairs. "You headed down?"

"Sure," I say.

And just like that, we start to walk downstairs together. It's hard for me to conceive of it—the head of the football team and me walking together through school. Surreal.

"What's your name?" O. says.

"Andy."

"I'm O."

He says it like I haven't heard of him. Like the whole school hasn't. In one way it's ridiculous, but it's also kind of cool that he doesn't just assume I would know him.

"Hold up a sec," he says when we get to the bottom of the stairs.

He licks his fingers and starts to nervously fix his hair. It reminds me of an actor getting ready to go onstage. After a couple seconds he says, "Ready."

And we walk out into the hall.

There are kids everywhere—talking, laughing, and splitting into groups before heading for their various clubs. The minute we step out, people begin to say hi to O. Not just a few people. Practically everybody. I'm used to walking down the hall without really being seen—fat but invisible—but O. is like a celebrity. Some people call his name, others nod, still others stop to ask him how he's doing. He negotiates it effortlessly, moving in a straight line while everyone reacts around him. He seems comfortable with it all, except I notice he reaches up and checks his hair from time to time.

I check a lot more than that. I make sure my fly is up and my stomach is sucked in. I hold my head up a little so it doesn't accentuate my double chin. Mom taught me that one.

But then an amazing thing starts to happen. I begin to feel like I'm taller. Thinner, too. I know I haven't changed in the last ten minutes, but I feel different. I walk with my shoulders up, and I nod at people I've never met in my life. All this just from standing next to O.

Just as I'm starting to enjoy myself, a guy with a thick neck cuts between us. He gives O. some kind of triple handshake that ends with them bumping fists.

The Neck notices me standing there.

"What do you want?" he says.

"We were talking," O. says.

"Right. Whatever." He turns away from me. "You ready to kick ass and take names?" he asks O.

"Let's do it," O. says.

O. nods to me once, and then he's off, walking side by side with the Neck. Actually, it's less like walking than it is strutting. They own the hall. People move out of the way to let them by.

I'm so stunned by what just happened, I stand and stare.

There's a group of people stopped at the end of the hall waiting for them. Lisa Jacobs and crew. The popular girls. One of the girls reaches down to unzip her backpack, and I see April.

O. slides into the middle of that crowd, and they all greet

each other. He even says hello to April. It's not like they hug and kiss, but I'm amazed they even know each other. How did April get to Hello Level with O.? A week ago she was at You Don't Exist Level.

I'm too far away to hear what anyone's saying. I watch it all like a scene through a window. April nervous, shifting from foot to foot, playing with her hair and smiling a lot.

Suddenly I feel sick to my stomach.

Eytan walks up doing a stiff-legged march and singing something unintelligible. I cover my ears.

"What the hell is that?" I say.

"Estonian National Anthem," he says in a thick accent. "We must hurry—glorious future UN triumph awaits."

"Okay, Borat."

Eytan pulls me down the hall towards the auditorium. Usually he's a pretty cool character, but today he's so excited he's practically skipping. I look back at O.'s group down at the opposite end of the hall.

"For what purpose do you suspend forward movement?" Eytan says.

"I have to go to the can," I say.

"There's no time for Number 2 when the fate of our Number 1 country hangs in the balance."

"It will be the fastest dump in history," I say.

He looks at me through squinted eyes. "You'd better set a land speed record," he says.

"I'll bring you the digital readout."

He pats me on the elbow and runs towards the auditorium.

I stand there for a minute. I don't really have to go to the bathroom. I just need a second to breathe.

I look back and forth down the hall. It's one of those moments when you know something big is happening, but you don't know what it is yet.

If I turn left, I'll follow Eytan to the Model UN meeting. Those are my people, the UN geeks. Any kind of geeks, really. I know what's going on in there, and it might even be fun. I can talk in a stupid accent like Eytan and try to score with the High Commissioner for Human Rights.

The thing is, I don't really like Model UN. I've never really told anyone.

Still, I belong there. I belong on the left.

I turn right.

Before I know it, I'm speed walking down the hall, doing my best to catch up to O. and his group without making it too obvious.

Maybe it's because of April. Maybe I'm just sick of being me. Or maybe it's something bigger. I don't know.

The hall leads all the way to the back of the school. I can see sunlight pouring in through the back door. I've never even gone out the back door. I've got nothing to do back there.

Until now.

O. and his posse crash through the door to the outside, and a minute later, I follow.

the secret world behind the school.

The field is crowded with people I don't know, all hanging around and talking to each other. I feel like I've wandered into something top secret. I imagine one of those horror films where everyone at school is slowly turning into aliens, and there's one guy who doesn't know about it until it's too late. He's walking towards danger while the audience is screaming, "Don't go out there, you idiot!"

I'm that idiot.

A whistle blows over to my left, and about twenty-five of the hottest, most popular girls in school crowd into a circle around the dance teacher. One of them pinwheels her arms like she's doing a cheer.

Cheer tryouts. Duh.

Maybe I'm not such an idiot after all.

April is there, too, biting nervously at her lip. April wants to be a cheerleader? It makes no sense.

On the other side of the field, about forty guys fall into rows in front of Coach Bryson. Coach looks at them while he spins a football on his finger.

Football. Cheerleaders. This is *Twilight Zone* stuff.

I walk over to the group of football jocks gathering around Coach. He does a double take when he sees me. He stops twirling the football and starts twirling the corner of his moustache.

"You gotta be yanking my yak," Coach says. "What do you want, Zansky?"

"I want to play football," I say.

Forty guys look at me like I'm crazy. Thirty-nine, actually. O. Douglas looks at me a little differently. He has a half smile on his face, like he's kind of curious.

"Uh—look, Zansky," Coach says, "have you ever played football before?" He says it like I'm a little kid.

"He only plays soccer," a goofy-looking guy says, and everyone laughs. Jurassic Pork. Hysterical.

"Have you even touched a football?" Coach says.

I think about Dad and me on the quad at Harvard, throwing a ball around. He started taking me there when I was eight, hoping I'd get a taste for football and Ivy. Instead I got a taste for the warm rolls at Bertucci's.

"I can throw a little," I tell Coach. Throwing was always easy. It's catching that was the problem.

The girls' cheer rings across the field:

N-E-W-T/
Add O-N-S and you will see/
How lizards fight for victory!

"You have to let him try out," a Latino guy says. "Equal opportunity and all that."

He has a line of facial hair that starts above his nose then winds its way all over his face like he was attacked by a Sharpie marker. It's not really a moustache. More of a facestache.

"Yeah," a short, thick guy with acne says. "You remember that girl who wanted to wrestle in Wisconsin?"

"If girls wrestled, I'd be wearing tights and grabbing guys' asses," the goofy guy says.

The acne guy says, "You tired of wrestling with your mother, Cheesy?"

"Not tired," Cheesy says. "I'm just looking to expand my dating horizons."

A bunch of guys laugh. All except that guy with the thick neck. The Neck just stares at me, expressionless. He's got white sweatbands pulled up above his elbows that make his arms look massive.

Coach looks at me and sighs.

"I just want to try," I say. It sounds feeble, even to me.

"We all deserve one chance to fail," Facestache says.

"Rico Suave is right," a huge black guy says. "Even girls get to try out."

Coach has had enough: "Rodriguez, Cheesy, Bison—all of you. Haul ass!"

He blows a double tap on the whistle and the guys break into a run, circling around the perimeter of the field.

Coach steps towards me. He pats his belly like he's petting a dog. "You sure you're up for this, son?"

I'm not sure of anything. But with April behind me, the jocks in front of me, and Ugo back where I came from, it's an excellent time to lie.

go.

It begins with running, moves on to calisthenics, and then it really gets ugly. I'm struggling along as best I can, sneaking sips on my inhaler when nobody is looking. But who am I kidding? I can't do any of this stuff. My idea of sports is Grand Theft Auto. I can run for hours on that, and I'm not tired at all. At worst I have a thumb cramp.

In the pause between drills, O. quickly introduces me around. The guy with the bad jokes is Cheesy. Facestache is Rodriguez, aka Rico Suave. The big black guy is Frison, aka Bison. Everyone has a nickname. Except me.

I barely exist. Guys won't even nod when they meet me, much less say my name. They just stare, challenging me. Everyone looks like they're ready to fight.

I glance at my watch. It's been six minutes, and it feels like I've been out here for ten years.

I'll be honest. Model UN is sounding better and better.

We set up for a sled drill. The sled is this thing that weighs about three million pounds. Coach blows his whistle and six guys at a time run and slam into them.

When you watch football on TV, people bang into things all the time. They even put mics down on the field so you hear the *crack* when the bodies hit. No big deal, right?

Very big deal.

It hurts.

We're supposed to hit the sleds hard enough to push them backwards. Guys scream and crash into them without blinking. When it's my turn, I try to do the same, only when I hit the sled for the first time, it's like running into a wall. Every bone in my body hurts.

I limp back to the line, panting and clutching my chest.

"Die on your own time," Rodriguez says.

"I'm not dying," I say. But I can't be too sure.

Coach blows the whistle again.

"Get some!" Rodriguez screams, and he hits the same sled I bounced off of and moves it back about four feet. He steps away and surveys the distance with a frown.

"I suck," he says.

"There's always girls' softball," Cheesy says.

"I've got experience with big balls," Rodriguez says, and grabs his crotch.

"So does your mother," Cheesy says, and grabs his crotch, too.

The mother stuff again. Unbelievable. These guys are obsessed.

I give the sled another try, imitating Rodriguez's run style, but when I hit, there's no crack. There's a thud, and I bounce off again.

"Good hustle," Coach says. He says it like it's a good thing, but he's got a look on his face like Dad used to get when I played T-ball. I'd swing and miss the ball, and Dad would sigh and look away.

As I'm walking back to the line, O. puts his hand on my shoulder and walks with me.

"These guys are not just running at the sled," he says.

"What are they doing?"

O. pauses like he's thinking of a way to explain it to me.

"Do you ever get angry?" he says.

"All the time," I say.

"Not just angry. Seriously pissed off. Like you want to hurt someone."

"I guess."

"That's the secret. You have to go to that place and spend a little time there," he says.

I want to ask him more, but he peels away to set up for the next drill.

No more sleds. Coach has us form two lines and face each other man-to-man.

"Look at the man across from you," Coach says.

I'm standing opposite Cheesy. He's got the sweatbands on his arms, too. He pulls them up across thick muscles.

"This man is not your friend," Coach says. "He is an interloper, an invader of your private territory. He is the son of a bitch who eats the last ice-cream sandwich from the freezer without replacing the box."

"Get some!" Rodriguez screams.

"You will push this man back," Coach says. "You will protect the ice-cream sandwich."

The guys *grunt* loudly.

Cheesy leans towards me. "Jurassic Pork," he says. "You ain't so tough when you get around the real dinosaurs."

"Set!" Coach says.

O. said I had to go to that place. What is that place?

I think about someone eating my ice-cream sandwich. That's irritating. Then I think of a tray of Mom's mini muffins, wanting them, but Mom saying I can't have them. That kind of makes me mad.

I think about Dad all alone in an apartment in downtown Boston.

I think about Justin with his arm around April's shoulders the other day.

My jaw clenches and I bite down hard.

I think about walking through the cafeteria, how my fat makes me feel like some giant Jell-O mold that everyone laughs at when it shakes.

"Go!" Coach says.

I explode off the line, crashing head-on into Cheesy. I hit and bounce, and then I slap and hit again like I see the guys doing. Coach blows the whistle to stop. I look at the line and realize I'm exactly where I started. I haven't pushed forward, but I haven't been pushed back.

"All right!" Cheesy says. "A little challenge. Me likey."

It's the exact opposite of what I expected. I thought Cheesy would be angry with me for banging into him. I assumed fighting back would get you killed like it does in the hall with Ugo, but the rules are different out here.

"Reset!" Coach says.

I glance over to the girls, and I catch a blur of hair and moving limbs. More things I can't have.

"Go!" Coach says. "Go, go, go, go—"

I roar and leap at Cheesy, only he's not Cheesy anymore. He's Mom/Dad/Jessica/Justin all rolled into one. I attack, pushing, grunting, and swinging my arms. I can't see the field or any of the players. I can't even see Cheesy in front of me.

Before I know what's happening, O. and a bunch of guys are pulling me back by the waist. Cheesy has his arms up like he's trying to surrender, and I'm hitting him. There's a piece of torn fabric in my hand. One of Cheesy's armbands.

"You stop when I blow the damn whistle!" Coach says.

"I didn't hear it," I say.

"Dude," Cheesy says. "It's just practice. Take it easy on my bands." He rubs his arm where I ripped the sweatband off him.

Bison steps up like he's going to beat the crap out of me. "You want me to school the boy?" he says.

O. jumps into the middle of things. He pats Bison on the shoulder and motions for him to back away. He checks to make sure Cheesy is okay. Then he turns his attention back to me.

"Let's grab a Gator," he says.

He walks me towards a red tank.

"Everything copasetic?" he says.

"I did what you said. I went to that place."

"No kidding," O. says.

He takes a shot of red liquid, offers one to me.

"Now we have to teach you how to get back," he says.

how not to limp in front of your mom.

"I'm going to take a bath," I tell Mom when I get home.

"You don't take baths," Mom says.

"I'm in the mood. So kill me," I say.

"Don't get angry with me," Mom says.

"I'm not angry," I say.

But I am angry. I feel like breaking something. Maybe it's because of football. You get used to hitting things. It's hard to stop.

Also, I'm pissed off about the end of practice. I can't shower in the locker room because it's one of those group showers where everyone can see you. That's not showering; that's a Public Display of Fatness. Definitely not an option. So when the guys started to get undressed and put on those little towels, I flew out the door.

"Do you want some bath salts?" Mom says when I'm half-way up the stairs.

"I love bath salts," Jessica shouts from the den. Eaves-dropping as usual.

"I'll run the water for you," Mom says, and she shoots up the stairs.

Very strange.

I walk upstairs slowly, trying hard not to limp in front of Mom. My body feels like it was put through a medieval torture chamber. I saw a special about that on the History Channel. In medieval times they would torture you, throw you into a dungeon, and feed you gruel. The narrator said "gruel" like it was a bad thing, but on the TV show, the gruel looked a lot like oatmeal. I wouldn't mind eating oatmeal several times a day. Unless Mom ran the dungeon. Then I'd probably get mini gruel.

When I go into the bathroom, Mom is stirring purple salt into the water with her hand.

"I don't want to smell like flowers," I say.

"It's not flowers," Mom says. "It's lavender."

"Lavender is a flower, Mom."

"Since when?"

"Look at the label," I say.

She holds up the bottle. There's a picture of a purple flower.

"Well, what do you know?" she says. "Forty years and I never knew what lavender was!"

That makes me laugh. Mom laughs a little, too. She hasn't done that in a while.

"I've been hard on you lately, haven't I?" Mom says.

"No," I say, even though the answer is yes.

I check the flap on my robe to make sure Mom can't see my underwear. The tag says ONE SIZE FITS ALL, but I must be larger than "ALL" because the robe doesn't fit me too well anymore.

Mom says, "You've been helping me out so much at events—I don't know what I'd do without you."

It's small in the bathroom and we're almost touching. The smell of lavender makes me a little woozy.

"I worry about your weight," Mom says. "That's why I'm on you so much."

"It's okay, Mom. Really." I don't want to have this conversation for the ten-thousandth time.

"I know what it's like to be a heavy child. Especially in high school. Kids can be cruel."

I've seen pictures of Mom from her senior year. She wasn't exactly fat, but she had chipmunk cheeks, and she looks uncomfortable in front of the camera. I can always tell when someone looks uncomfortable. It's my special gift. Probably because I'm so uncomfortable.

"Maybe I'm a bad mother."

"You're not a bad mother."

"Then why won't you listen to me? If I was a good mother, I'd be able to get through to you. Other mothers get through."

"No, they don't."

"The good mothers do."

"Trust me. They don't."

I can't tell if Mom's crying, or if it's just the steam from the bath making her cheeks red.

"It's going to be okay," I say.

"It's *my* job to say things like that," Mom says.

Mom smoothes down my hair, and I wince. I can't help it. I don't like to be touched.

"I hope you have the best year ever," Mom says.

Mom wipes her eyes. I think she really was crying.

She pauses at the door. "I know you talk to your father during the week," she says.

I pull the belt on my robe into a tight knot.

"No, I don't," I say.

"Well, if you do, you might just mention . . . he's a month behind with the check."

Mom has this amazing ability to ruin any moment. I thought Mom was being nice to me because she wanted to give me a pep talk. Now I feel like I got set up.

Mom says, "We're trying to avoid going to court. To keep things friendly, you know."

"I know," I say.

"So if you mention it to him, that would help a lot."

"Fine," I say.

"You're not angry, are you?"

"Of course not."

Mom closes the door. I get in the stupid tub that smells like flowers. The water scorches my skin, but it feels good on my muscles, too. Pain and pleasure at the same time. Like buffalo wings. Like high school.

how to lie to your best friend.

I'm hanging around outside AP History, pretending to tie my shoe for the eighteenth time. I've been waiting for April for ten minutes, all the time pretending I'm not. Love at second sight is a lot of work. That's what I'm starting to think.

I bend over again, and I feel my pants ride down my butt.

"Attractive," Eytan says from behind me.

"It's the Eighth Wonder of the World," I say.

"Eighth and Ninth," Eytan says.

"It's these stupid new pants. If I pull up the front, they fall down in back. If I pull up the back, my stomach pops out."

"It's the movement of the cosmos. Where something is born, something else dies."

Eytan adjusts his John Lennon glasses and stares at me.

"Speaking of ass—what happened to you yesterday?"

"Sorry about that," I say. "I had an emergency. I think a Russian agent slipped me something. Insta-poops."

"The Russians took your colon hostage?"

"Anything to prevent Estonia from rising."

Eytan eyes me suspiciously, but he knows that I really do get the runs a lot. You can't blame a guy for IBS.

Suddenly April walks by. Before I can say hello, Eytan swirls his arm in the air a bunch of times and bows deeply from the waist.

"Good day to you, madam," he says in a fake British accent.

April doesn't answer, just walks by with her head down.

"Ouch," Eytan says. "Is my Jew-'fro singed?"

"It's not you. I'm still socially radioactive. She saw that soccer game."

We go into class together. April is sitting alone on the other side of the room next to the pencil sharpener. If I have to sit through a whole class watching Justin try to flirt with her, I'll kill myself.

I have to do something.

That's when a crazy thought occurs to me. If I can face off against Cheesy, I should be able to talk to a girl for two minutes.

I drop my books on the desk next to Eytan, hold my pencil by my side, and snap the point off with my thumbnail. "I'm going to sharpen this bad boy up," I say.

I walk across the room, silently praying for my ass crack to stay under wraps. As I pass April's desk, I chicken out. I don't say a word. I just stick my pencil in the sharpener and start grinding away. It gets shorter and shorter while my mind whirls. Freud would have a heyday with this one.

"I saw you on the field yesterday," April says out of the blue.

"Really?" I say. I pretend I didn't notice her sitting right there.

"How'd you do?"

"I did great," I say. "Not at all like that stupid soccer game last week."

I mime my shorts falling down. She looks shocked at first, but then she laughs. It's a big risk reminding her of that day, but that's what the guys on the team do. When they make a mistake, they're not shy about it. They make fun of themselves, and it makes everything better.

"How'd the cheerleading go?" I say.

"Great," she says. She bites at her lower lip. "Actually, not so good. I'm really out of shape, you know?"

I glance down at her legs. I can't help it. She's wearing a skirt, and I can see her thigh muscles. They're tight and muscular, which has me wondering about her definition of "out of shape."

"I might get cut," she says.

"No way. You have nothing to worry about. I was watching you."

"You were?"

I feel my face turning red. I don't want her to think I'm a stalker or something.

"Were my jumps high enough?" she says. She tugs nervously at an errant piece of hair.

"They were really high," I say.

"The girls didn't say anything."

"Maybe they're jealous."

April laughs. "What do they have to be jealous about?"

Ms. Hartwell clears her throat. "Let's get started," she says.

"See you soon," April whispers.

I walk across the room with my stubby little pencil, and I notice everyone's looking at me. That's probably because I'm the ballsy guy who made April laugh. Or maybe it's because my pants are riding low again.

"I thought you were radioactive," Eytan says when I get back.

"I guess my reactor has been contained," I say.

Eytan looks at April. "Are you putting your rod in the core?"

"Of course not." I feel my cheeks getting hot.

Eytan crosses his arms. "I don't know what's going on with you, but I'm going to figure it out."

Ms. Hartwell flips on the overhead projector. She stands framed in the spotlight.

I glance across the room, and April smiles at me.

"War breaks out in Lexington," Ms. Hartwell says, "and it all begins with one, unexpected shot."

back in the big leagues.

I'm rolling a kickball to a girl in a scoliosis brace while Warner looks on and smiles. I want to elbow him in the head. What is there to be happy about?

Suddenly Coach pops through the door of the gym. A ripple of fear passes through the Slow Gym kids. Coach might ask us to do something. Like stand up.

"Zansky!" He motions me over.

"Yeah, Coach?"

He puts an arm around my shoulders and whispers, "You don't need to be playing patty-cake in here, son. Why don't you come outside and join the party?"

"I don't know, Coach. I'm not too good at soccer."

Coach chuckles. "Tell you what," he says. "We'll put you on goal today. You can guard it rather than knock it down."

I look back at the Slow Gym kids. Warner is watching me, the little eyes in his big face staring. He's not smiling anymore.

He looks sort of pitiful, like those puppies in the store window at the mall when you walk away from them. I want to punch him for looking at me like that.

"What do you say?" Coach asks.

"Good idea," I say.

I walk onto the field and the game stops dead. The whole class turns at the same time to watch me. A guy in an ankle brace gives me a dirty look. One of my unfortunate victims.

April is talking to a cute blonde girl. They whisper to each other when they see me.

"It's the Thunder Down Under," Becky Samuelson says. Becky's dad is practically a movie star, so she thinks she's one, too. Anyway, her comment gets a big laugh.

I just stand there on the field with an empty ten-foot zone around me. It's like the time I had gas in temple.

"Take it easy on my bands!" someone shouts. It's Rodriguez from the football team, grinning and smoothing down his facestache. I didn't even know he was in this gym class.

"You're back in the big leagues, huh?" he says, and he gives me a rough handshake.

"I guess."

"Even great players go down to Triple-A sometimes. They work on the skill set until they get called up again."

Rodriguez head-butts a soccer ball. It rolls into the center of the field.

"*Vamanos*," he says.

We jog back onto the field. I kick the ball back and forth with Rodriguez for a minute. With the two of us together, nobody dares to say anything. They just form back into teams, and the game starts up like nothing ever happened.

A second later April runs by.

"Welcome back," she says, and she gives me a wink.

the elephant in the living room.

"When it's time for nominations, remember," Eytan says, "nothing below Commerce Secretary. It's degrading."

We're rushing down the hall towards the Model UN meeting. Eytan is wearing an old sports coat over a Radiohead T-shirt. Business attire.

"I'm not sure I want a position this semester," I say.

"What are you talking about?"

"I'm really busy. I may need to fade into the background."

"We're sophomores now," Eytan says. "No more fading."

What I don't say is that yesterday was the last day of football tryouts, and everyone's waiting for the list to go up. I keep trying to tell Eytan what's happening, but it never seems to be the right time. Maybe that's how it was with Dad and Miriam. He wanted to tell Mom, but he never found the right time.

We stop in front of a door with a handwritten sign: REPUBLIC OF ESTONIA.

"I really played you up during the meeting last week," he says, "so walk like you got a pair."

"A pair of what?"

"Massive Estonian gonads."

"Dude, I've got a lot on my mind," I say.

Eytan looks at me strangely. He says, "What's with the 'dude' stuff? Let's switch to polysyllabic mode, huh? We're heading into the diplomatic trenches."

He throws open the door.

I spend the rest of the afternoon discussing what Eytan calls the great balancing act—ways to protect our tiny republic without pissing off our giant and powerful neighbor, Russia. An hour in and we've switched to debating military strategy.

"Historically, diplomacy has proven to be an effective deterrent," Eytan says.

Justin leaps out of his seat.

"Why don't we just f-ing attack?" he says.

"It's true," another kid says. "The best defense is a good offense."

"We barely have an army," I say. "What are we going to attack with?"

"Nuke them," Justin says. "It's tough for dust to invade."

"That's crazy," I say.

"Let me get this straight," Justin says. "We're a tiny little do-nothing country, and we're going to trust this giant, powerful country not to screw us over?" He coughs and says, "Bullshit" at the same time.

Eytan stretches, completely unperturbed. He says, "What's your idea, Delegate Zansky?"

It's a softball pitch. He's setting me up to knock one out of the park.

Justin stands on one side of the room and I stand on the other. The Model UN geeks look from one to the other, waiting for fireworks.

This is my comfort zone. Geeks and obscure geopolitics. Two of my best subjects.

Anyway, it beats the hell out of getting pounded on the field by sweaty strangers. Here we pound each other with our brains.

"Well?" Justin says.

I stand up slowly. "Allow me to quote Sun Tzu: 'He will win who knows when to fight and when not to fight.'"

"What's that supposed to mean?" Justin says.

"We cooperate with them. We let peace be our war."

The geeks applaud. Eytan jumps out of his seat.

"Thank you, Delegate Zansky for that subtle and compelling analysis. Fellow delegates, it is my honor to nominate Andrew Zansky for Secretary of the Defense Committee."

"Second!" someone screams.

"I respectfully decline," I say.

"All in favor?" Eytan says, steamrolling me.

A resounding "Aye!" thunders through the room.

"Motion passes," Eytan says. "Congratulations, Mr. Zansky. The defense of the Republic now rests squarely on your shoulders."

the center of it all.

Friday afternoon. My stomach grumbles like it's filled with greasy Chinese food. I've been to the bathroom six times since this morning, and I haven't eaten a thing. Mom calls them the nervous poops.

Why am I nervous?

The list is going up at 1:00 and it's 12:59.

I'm walking towards the gym when Nancy Yee intercepts me.

"I heard a rumor that you were going out for football," Nancy says.

She's wearing this crazy frock dress with old-lady shoes and socks that go up under her knees. I swear she's from a different planet.

"Don't believe everything you hear," I say.

"Do you know what happened on the team last year?"

"I know we won."

"We?" she says.

"The team. *Our* team. School pride. You've heard of that, right?"

We turn the corner and there's a huge crowd standing around the bulletin boards outside the gym. I have to ditch Nancy so I can look at the list. I don't want her to know anything about this. Plus April's down there, and I'm afraid she'll see us and get the wrong idea.

"Oh, shoot," I say, "I forgot something in my locker. I have to go all the way back up."

I'm hoping Nancy will go away, but she turns like she's attached to me. I've grown a barnacle. Unbelievable.

"Do you like her?" Nancy says.

"Who?"

"The new girl."

"Which new girl?"

Nancy sighs. "The Korean girl," she says.

"She's really smart."

"That's not what I asked."

Nancy hooks her bangs with two fingers and pulls them tight behind her ears. Her acne glares at me angrily.

"I have to go," she says, and runs up the stairs. Barnacle removed.

"What's your problem?" I say, but it's not like I go after her. Honestly, it's a relief that she's gone. Now I can go where the action is. Down the hall.

There are two bulletin boards on the wall, each with a clump of students around them, jocks on one side and cheerleaders on the other. If I saw a group like this last year, I'd run in the other direction. Now I'm right in the middle of them. Welcome to the new world order.

I stand behind the jocks, afraid to get too close to the piece of paper. What if my name is on it? What if it's not? And why do jocks do this whole thing in public? Couldn't they send the results to your house like the SAT? At least then you could fail in the privacy and comfort of your own bedroom.

O. Douglas comes down the hall and casually walks to the front of the crowd. He glances at the paper, grins, then steps back.

"How'd you do?" Cheesy says.

"Made it," O. says, and brushes his forehead like he's wiping away sweat. Everyone laughs. The funny thing is that he actually sounds relieved, like it's possible he might have been cut.

"Get up there," Rodriguez says to me. "Don't you want to know?"

"Not really," I say.

He pushes me towards the front of the crowd, and the guys split down the middle to let me through.

I break into a sweat. An old prayer from Hebrew school pops into my head. I say it silently, and then I remember it's the prayer for bread. Fabulous. I know one prayer, and it's for *challah*.

The list is in alphabetical order. I brace myself. Thirty

seconds of public shame, and then I can slink back into the obscurity of Estonian ephemera. I follow the names with my finger, all the way to the bottom where I see:

ZANSKY, ANDREW— CENTER

Holy sweet mother. The bread prayer worked.

"Center what?" I say.

"Center position," Rodriguez says.

"What's that mean?"

"That means it's you and me," O. says. He mimes like I'm hiking the ball, and he's grabbing and throwing.

"No friggin' way," I say.

The guys laugh. A bunch of them slap me on the back.

"Welcome to the Offense, baby," Bison says.

"Now you're part of the O-Line," Rodriguez says, and the guys grunt and bump chests.

I stand there wide-eyed, taking it all in.

"It's a rush, isn't it?" O. says.

I move to the back of the hall, standing with the guys who made it. I notice a few guys who check the list, then walk away really upset. It's like Dad says—there are winners and losers in the world, it just depends which side fate decides to put you on. Maybe that's why I feel strange right now. I've always been on the other side. I mean I'm a winner in Model UN and on English tests, but that's not really winning. That's like the consolation prize they give a loser on a game show so he doesn't drive his car into a telephone pole on his way home.

A group of girls scream, and April pops out of the circle of cheerleaders with a big smile on her face. Lisa Jacobs gives her a huge hug. April laughs and snaps her fingers as she dances a kooky dance. Korean girl gone wild. I wave to her across the hall, and she comes over to me.

"Hey," she says. "Did you make the team?"

"You're talking to the new center," I say.

"What's the center do?"

"I'll let you know in about a week."

April laughs. "Well, I guess we're going to be seeing a lot of each other," she says.

Lisa Jacobs rushes past and jumps into O.'s arms. They start making out like crazy two feet away from April and me, sucking face so loud it sounds like a kid drinking from the bottom of a juice container.

"Celebratory tongue," April says.

"Delicious," I say.

"And low in calories."

I'm hoping April will be overcome with emotion and give me some celebratory tongue. Instead she rolls her eyes.

Suddenly a girl screams and bursts into tears over by the list.

"That's so sad," April says.

"Not everyone has what it takes."

"That's kind of a jerky thing to say."

She's right. I do sound like a jerk. It's just that when you're laughing and joking with the winners, it's hard to care too much about the losers. They kind of fade into the background.

"Sorry about that," I say. "I meant that you deserve it. You worked really hard. And you're great."

"That's sweet," she says. "Thanks, Andrew."

She smiles at me, but no tongue.

"Get it while it's hot," the Neck says. He walks through the crowd handing out papers. He gives me one, but he looks in the other direction like I'm not there.

The top of the paper says: *Consent to Participate in Intramural Athletics.*

"What's this?" I ask Cheesy.

"No big deal," he says. "You have to have your folks sign it."

"Why?"

"In case you die. They can't sue the school." He laughs.

"Shut up, fool," Rodriguez tells him.

Cheesy says to me, "I was just kidding, dude. Don't get your sack in a knot."

I read quickly through the consent form. I'm not thinking about dying. I'm thinking about something much worse.

Living.

There's no way Mom is going to sign the form. Which means I'm going to be the first guy in history who makes the football team and can't play because his Mommy won't let him. When that gets around, I'm going to be what Eytan calls an NSG.

No Sex Guaranteed.

hurry plus.

I'm sitting in Finagle Bagels with the iPhone to my ear, waiting for Dad to come on the line. I take a deep breath. Is there anything that smells better than baking bread? It's as close to heaven as you can get in this world. It's like the air loves you.

"Everything okay?" Dad says after his secretary puts me through.

Dad's got that "hurry" tone in his voice. He almost always has that hurry tone, but when he's in the office, it's like hurry plus, as if he expects you to kick it into high gear.

"I need to talk to you about school," I say.

"How's that going?"

"The year is off to a great start."

"Great start, huh?" Dad's voice perks up. "You have a girlfriend, don't you?"

"Not exactly."

"You sly dog. You have two. You're playing the end against the middle."

I want to hang up. I want to tell Dad I can't talk to him anymore, that I'm out of minutes for the month.

"Like father like son," I hear Dad saying, but I missed what he said before that.

"I have some good news, Dad. I'm playing football this year."

"You in a weekend league or something?"

"Varsity football."

There's silence on the line.

"I don't know what to say, Andrew. This is . . . stupendous news."

"You have to come to games."

"Absolutely." Dad pauses. "Did I hear you correctly? You said 'varsity'?"

"Varsity. That's right."

"Son of a gun. I wouldn't have guessed that in a million years." Dad calls out to the office: "My son made varsity!"

I hear people congratulating him in the background. Great news. You've got a jock now.

"I need a favor, Dad."

"You want some equipment money?"

That reminds me of what Mom said about the check. But now is not the time.

"I need you to sign a form," I say.

Dad's voice instantly changes. "What kind of form?"

He sounds suspicious. Dad's an attorney. He doesn't sign forms without a million questions.

"It's a consent form," I say. "Giving me permission to play."

"What did your mother say about this?"

"She doesn't know yet. I wanted to tell you first."

I smile, even though Dad can't see me. I read a *Psychology Today* article that said your voice changes when you smile, and people are more inclined to believe you.

"What about your asthma?" Dad says.

"Not an issue."

"You're sure."

"More than sure," I say.

I take another deep breath so Dad can hear how clear my lungs are. I catch a whiff of bagels fresh from the oven. Ten seconds later a tray of hot sesame bagels comes out of the back. My nose is a genius. No doubt about it.

The girl holds the bagels over the wire rack and shakes, and they drop into the bin. I reach for my wallet.

"I'll be happy to sign the form," Dad says. "As long as your mother agrees."

"She agrees."

"You just said you haven't told her."

"I meant she will agree."

I walk up to the counter. I point at the hot bagels and make a "two" sign with my fingers. I know I shouldn't, but I can't help myself.

Dad says, "I don't need any problems, Andrew. There's already enough tension in this family."

"There won't be any problems."

"Cream cheese?" the girl says.

"No," I say silently. I love cream cheese, but with a hot bagel, it's just distracting.

Dad says, "All right then. Have your mom sign it, then I'll sign it."

"Thanks, Dad."

Dad doesn't say good-bye. That's a waste of money. His picture simply goes from big to tiny on my iPhone. Call over.

I bite into the first bagel, feel the crunch as my teeth pass through the crust into the soft, hot dough beneath. I know I've got problems, but I can't worry about them now. Right now my mouth is busy, and that makes life seem good.

mini miracle required.

It's six o'clock, and Mom's cooking mini sausages for a party tomorrow. Sometimes she cooks right through dinner, turning down the heat briefly, running over to the table to take a few bites, then running back to the kitchen to stir. She says it relaxes her. It makes the rest of us tense.

"How was UN?" Mom asks.

"Incredible," I say. "I'm heading up the Defense Committee."

I feel my stomach turn over. I haven't figured out how I'm going to handle that little issue yet. My bowels might get me out of one or two UN sessions, but an entire semester? I'd have to take a dump the size of Faneuil Hall and make a video to prove it to Eytan.

Mom lifts a sausage to her mouth, blows on it twice, then thinks better of it. She holds it out to me on the end of a fork.

"Are these too spicy?" she says.

I pop the sausage in my mouth and feel the burst of hot grease. It's sweet with an overlay of spicy. Mom at her very best.

"It's perfect," I say. "You're perfect."

"Thank you, sweetie." Mom giggles like a little girl. She loves a compliment almost as much as Jessica.

"What do you think about sports, Mom?"

"Your grandmother had a cancerous mole removed. You can't be too careful."

"What are you talking about?"

"Spots. You have to be vigilant. Cancer runs in our family," Mom says.

"I said *sports*, Mom. You know, like tennis?"

"Please, Andrew. I know what tennis is."

"What do you think about me playing sports?"

The pan sizzles. Mom shakes it hard.

"What sport do you want to play?" Mom says.

"Something that would help me get some exercise."

"You mean like bowling?"

"Bowling, baseball, whatever."

"What about your asthma?"

The asthma again. My whole family is waiting for me to die. Unbelievable.

"I haven't had an asthma attack in years," I say.

Not a full-scale one, at least. Mini ones. Two puffs on the

inhaler and I'm fine. But I don't want Mom to remember any of that.

"I don't know," Mom says. "It worries me."

Mom removes the sausages, placing them on paper towels to drain the fat. I wish I could drain my fat. I'd lay on a giant, triple-absorbent towel at 306.4 lbs., then stand up at 180.

"I want to play so I can lose some weight," I say. "That's all it is."

It's hard for Mom to argue with reasoning like that.

"Why don't you try walking to school in the mornings?" Mom says.

"I hate walking to school."

"My point is, you don't have to play sports in order to lose weight. You could do something less dangerous. Maybe you could work out with your sister."

Jessica speed walks around the neighborhood. Mom doesn't know it, but she puts weights on her ankles under her pants so she'll burn extra calories. Sometimes she wears them in the house, too, but she puts her socks over them so we won't notice.

"Forget it," I say. "I'm sorry I asked."

"Don't yell at me," Mom says. "I'm worried about you. Remember, I'm the one who rushed you to the hospital when you had an attack."

"That was when I was eight!"

"You had to get an emergency shot of adrenaline. Remember?"

"I remember."

"Your father wasn't around. He was working. No surprise. But I was there, Andy. I saw what can happen."

Mom drops raw, pink pork into the pan and it sizzles in protest.

I have the consent form in my back pocket, but I don't even bother to take it out.

wide awake and dreaming.

"Slow your roll," Coach says as I jog onto the field. He holds out his hands like he wants something.

"What?" I say.

"I didn't get your form. In my mailbox by ten a.m., latest. That's what I told you."

"I forgot it at home."

"You forgot it, huh?" Coach scratches his chin. "What else are you going to forget?"

"Nothing."

"Are you going to forget to show up for games?"

"No."

"Will you forget the plays?"

I don't know what the plays are, but I say, "No, Coach."

"Maybe you'll forget to protect your quarterback? The bad men will come running at you, and you'll start to breathe fast and your little heart will go pitter-patter in your chest, and you'll forget that you're a football player. Is that what I can expect from you?"

"Absolutely not."

"The form is signed, right?"

"Of course."

"Bring it tomorrow," Coach says.

"Will do," I say.

But there's no way I can bring it tomorrow. Mom won't sign, and Dad won't sign without Mom. Maybe Coach will get busy with other things and he'll forget. Maybe I can stage a *Mission Impossible*–style break-in, steal the file cabinet, and drop it in the Charles. Maybe we'll have a late season nor'easter and the school will be destroyed—

"Zansky!"

"What is it, Coach?"

"Wake up, son. I'm talking to you."

"I'm wide awake."

"You don't have the epilepsy, do you? My cousin's son had the epilepsy. The boy used to fall asleep on his feet. One time he rode his bike off the side of a parking garage, didn't know it until he hit the ground."

"It's not epilepsy. I just think a lot."

"You know what thinking does to a football player? It gets you killed. I don't need you thinking. I need situational awareness."

"I'll work on it," I say.

"That's the right attitude. Now get out there."

out there.

Do you know what a center does?

Get this.

I crouch down like a sumo wrestler, take the ball in my right hand while I lean on my left knee. O. Douglas bends over behind me, and he kind of puts his knuckles up against my butt, and he screams a whole bunch of numbers until he gets to *"Hike!"* It doesn't even sound like "hike" when he says it. He has his own style. Something more like *"Haaa-eeee!"*

A guy puts his hands on your ass and screams, *"Haaa-eeee!"* What would your reaction be?

Run like hell. Call the cops.

That's not what the center does. The center leans back, leans into it. When O. screams, that's my cue. I lift the ball, twist, and push it up and into his hands. That's the snap.

O. says the snap is the starting point of all things. It's the trigger of the gun.

But there's one other little part to it. While I'm crouched down, there's a huge, ugly guy standing three inches in front of me, waiting to kill me. The second the ball leaves my hands that guy smashes into my head.

Football. Good times.

Today after calisthenics and running, we set up for snap-and-pass drills. O. calls out some numbers then screams, *"Haaa-eeee!"* I snap the ball back . . . but instead of going into his hands, I fling it right past him onto the ground.

"Crap," I say.

"Relax," O. says. "You'll get it."

O. calls another play. I snap again. This time I feel a crunch as the ball bangs into the tips of his fingers. I see the Neck shaking his head like I'm a lost cause.

Maybe I am.

The cheerleaders are working out over on the soccer field. It's impossible not to keep looking over there. They're wearing short skirts and jumping up and down. The other players look a little bit, but they're subtle about it. They don't really look, they glance. That's the difference between guys who get girls and guys who don't.

Cool guys glance. Geeks gawk. Two seconds too long, and you'll be spending your Saturday nights with a box of Kleenex. That's the cruel reality of high school.

"Where's your head at?" O. says.

"Right here," I say. It's just on the wrong field.

I snap the ball and almost break O.'s fingers again. He

snatches it away and calls a time-out. Then he walks me to the sideline.

"What's the plan?" O. says.

"I want to play football."

"The real plan," he says. "What's the real plan?"

A cheerleader screams. I look over to see April flying into the air, thrown aloft by two girls in short skirts.

O. catches me looking. "Got it," he says.

"That's not the plan," I say.

"Girls are great," O. says, "but here's the thing. When you're on this field, the guys are depending on you. I'm depending on you."

I reach for my inhaler. I don't suck it, just hold on to it in my sweatpants pocket. It makes me feel better knowing it's there if I need it.

"Can people depend on you?"

"Sure," I say.

"Prove it," O. says.

He hands me the ball.

"Maybe I'm no good at this," I say.

"Don't force it," O. says. "You have to find the rhythm. It's like dancing. You know how to dance, right?"

I think of the dozens of weddings I've been to, all the couples I've seen dancing. It feels like I've danced a million times, but when I really think about it, I realize I've never actually danced. I've only watched other people do it.

"No," I say.

"It's time to learn," O. says.

O. screams, *"Go again!"* and everyone sets up. This time Bison leans down in front of me and stares into my eyes. This is not the smiling Bison. This is someone I haven't met yet. I feel O. lean over behind me, one hand pressed under me, the other patting the small of my back.

Suddenly I hear music in my head. At first I don't recognize it, and then I remember I heard it at the last wedding. "True Colors." A bad, wedding version of it.

Embarrassing.

But it relaxes me. I lighten my grip on the ball like O. taught me. I breathe. I listen to "True Colors" in my head.

"Haaa-eeee!" O. screams.

I push up and back, moving to the music, and I feel the energy of the ball transfer from me to O. It's effortless, as if the ball disappeared from my hands and I had nothing to do with it. Maybe this is what dancing is supposed to feel like.

I'm so excited about my discovery, I forget all about what comes next.

Bison comes next.

He crashes into me, squashing me to the ground, then jumps past me and tackles O. The ball pops out of O.'s hands, and Bison scrambles after it. There's a jumble of bodies, and then Bison appears, smiling, holding the ball over his head like a trophy. I glance to the sidelines, and Coach is cursing and slamming his fists against his thighs.

"What in God's name—*Zansky!* What are you doing to my quarterback?!"

Coach rubs his stomach like he has a cramp. "Let me tell you what your job is," Coach says. "You are a wall. You are impassible. You are the Great Friggin' Wall of China. Do you know how long the Great Friggin' Wall has stood, Zansky?"

"No, Coach," I say.

"Ten thousand two hundred and eighty-three friggin' years. Repelling all invaders. Do you have that kind of commitment?"

I'm pretty sure Coach has his dates wrong by about eight thousand years, but it's probably not a good idea to correct him now.

"I think so," I say.

"You *think* so? You're going to let some Mongolian son of a bitch jump the wall and take my fried rice?!" Coach screams.

All the guys are looking at me.

"Absolutely not, Coach!"

"Will you protect my rice for the long haul? Will you keep it safe for *ten thousand friggin' years?*"

"*Yes, I friggin' will!*"

Coach's voice drops back down to normal. "Well, then. That's all I wanted to know."

He blows his whistle. "Hit the showers, gentlemen."

The guys slowly unwind, taking off their helmets and moving towards the locker room.

Coach pats O. on the back. "Mr. Burch pulled me aside for a little chat," he says.

O.'s face darkens.

"I blew the quiz," O. says. "It was a one-time thing."

"We need you to do well this year."

"I'm handling it. Guaranteed."

"All right, then," Coach says. "I have to motate. There's a protein shake in the fridge with my name on it."

"Protein shake?" O. says.

Coach pats his belly. "Hey, I've got to maintain my girlish figure."

Coach is on some crazy diet where he drinks six protein shakes a day. I should introduce him to Mom. They could count calories together.

"Who's Burch?" I say when Coach is gone.

O. moves closer and lowers his voice. "He's my English teacher. I flunked English last year."

"No way."

"It's not my fault. Burch thinks that because he's a genius, everyone else should be, too. He makes us write these huge book reports. It's too much."

"I thought athletes got automatic As," I say.

"Maybe if you live in Texas or something. But it doesn't work like that here. If you flunk a class, you can't play. C-average minimum. That's the athletic contract."

"But you're playing this year."

"Coach convinced him to give me an incomplete and let me take the class again. That's why I have to do well."

Everyone's hanging out in the back of the school talking, but O. and I are still on the field. It's amazing how quiet it is with just the two of us out here.

"What if we helped each other?" I say.

"What's that mean?"

"Like I could be your English tutor, and you could help me with football."

"Like a football tutor."

"Why not?"

O. thinks about it for a minute. "Our secret, right?"

"Completely."

"It's an interesting idea," O. says.

clutch.

A day later I'm sitting in O.'s living room tutoring him on *Huckleberry Finn*.

I like the story of Huck, and I'm trying to get through to O. about it. I think he understands the basics, but every time I try to talk about themes, he gets confused.

"You're saying Huck and Jim are the same?" O. says.

"Not the same, but they have the same problem."

His eyes fuzz out like Jessica when *Project Runway* comes on.

"Think about it," I say. "Huck has everything, all the advantages, and he hates it. Jim has nothing and he hates that. So they're both trapped by the same system, just on different ends of it."

O.'s face lights up. "Kind of like you and me, huh?"

"What do you mean?"

"High school, dude. The system."

I look at O. sitting there, his stomach flat as a board. I

understand how I could be trapped. I mean, fat and high school don't exactly go together. Kind of like barbed-wire underpants. But O.?

"How are you trapped?" I say.

"Don't get me wrong," O. says. "I'm not complaining. Things are good. Absolutely. But sometimes—I don't know. People expect things from me, and I have to deliver or I'm screwed."

"Like your dad?" I say.

"No, he doesn't care so much."

"He doesn't want you to be a jock?"

"He's fine with it. I mean, he used to be a jock in high school, but I don't think he even remembers. He's not one of those guys who dreams of the golden days. More like the golden parachute."

"So who then?"

O. opens his arms. "The school," he says, and he spreads his fingers wide.

I think about that for a second. I feel like there's so much pressure on me. Mom and Dad, Eytan, they all want stuff from me. But then there's me. I'm always putting pressure on myself, trying to prove myself, be smarter, or thinner, or cooler. When you're fat, that just comes with the territory. You walk through the door like Babar the Elephant, you have a lot of ground to make up for. At least that's how I think of it.

But when I think of O.'s life, I realize it's not just about him. There's a whole team relying on him. There's an entire school expecting him to be something. That's like pressure on a whole different level.

"You still there, dude?" O. says.

"Yeah. I'm just thinking," I say. "You represent things to people. Like if you succeed, the entire school succeeds. Right?"

"Kind of, yeah. And if I fail—"

"Newton sucks royal ass."

"You got it."

"But check it out, O. I'm thinking how when we represent things to people, it's not really about us anymore. It's like it's their problem. Not ours."

O. rubs his head. "You're deep, dude."

"And wide, too."

"Wide's a good thing on the O-Line."

"I guess."

"Bigger is better," O. says. "Especially in football."

"And in boobies," I say.

"What do you know about boobies?"

"I know I like them. And I wouldn't mind touching one before I die."

O. laughs and flips *Huckleberry Finn* onto the table.

"All in time," he says. "But listen, my head is about to explode. You want to get out there and throw the ball around?"

"Yeah," I say. "Enough of this philosophizing crap. Let's bang into something and make it bleed."

"Easy, killer," O. says.

We begin with simple handoffs. O. teaches me how to grip the ball properly, curving my wrist so the laces are aligned when I hand it to him. He shows me the basic snap, the quick snap, and the long snap where he stands a few yards behind and I pitch it back to him.

"I can show you the basics in an afternoon," O. says. "But once you have them, there's only one thing left to do."

"What's that?" I say.

"Practice for about ten thousand hours."

"I guess we'd better get started," I say.

Inside the house when we were studying, O. was edgy, nervous, and uncomfortable, but the minute we start to play, his whole energy changes. He relaxes and his body does what it knows best. Run. Jump. That kind of thing.

I'm the exact opposite.

My body knows how to sit, eat Spicy Cheetos, and program TiVo.

So when I get into the squat, it all goes to hell really quickly. I can sense where O. is, but I don't know how to orient the ball right.

"Just do the dance," O. says.

"I'll try," I say.

I listen for the music, and after a minute, it comes. "True Colors." Only it's a waltz version. I imagine I'm dancing with April. Her hair swirls as we move.

I don't think about what I'm doing. I just snap the ball. Perfect.

Now it becomes a disco song. I snap a dozen times, each better than the next.

Now I'm listening to a version by The Killers. It sounds like it's playing through the wall from Jessica's bedroom. I snap again and again, fifty times in a row, feeling the energy transfer between O. and me, sensing him come towards me and drop back, always knowing where I should direct the ball.

We do snaps until my back is on fire, and I'm sweating right through my shirt. Usually I'd be nervous about it sticking to my body because then you can see my fat, but alone with O., I barely notice.

"Let's grab some Gator," O. finally says.

"That's probably a good idea," I say, "before I pass out."

"You're still getting into shape. Stick with it for a few weeks, and you'll see some real changes."

I imagine myself at 180 with a six-pack stomach. I peel off my shirt in gym class like I saw Rodriguez do, and the girls start to sweat.

O. opens a little cooler that he brought outside. "What's it going to be? Red or blue?"

I look at the bottles of Gatorade.

"Is there a difference?"

"The blue goes down easier."

"I'll take red."

O. smiles. He cracks two bottles of red, and we drink. I want to down the whole thing in one shot, but I know better. You have to pace yourself or you cramp up. I learned that the hard way.

O. moves his shoulder back and forth and winces.

"Are you hurt?" I say.

"Just a little tight," O. says. "My shoulder got jammed up last season. Nothing to worry about."

It never occurred to me that O. could get injured. It's stupid, but he seems sort of invulnerable, like a superhero.

"Why don't you ever change in the locker room?" O. asks. I must wince or something, because he says, "No big deal. I'm just wondering. A couple of the guys noticed."

"I don't know why," I say.

"Do you have a tiny wiener or something?"

"No way," I say.

The truth is it looks kind of small compared to my thighs. Then again, a garbage truck looks small compared to my thighs.

"I'm just not comfortable," I say.

"Being naked in front of people."

"Being naked anytime. I don't even like to take my clothes off when I'm alone in my room."

O. laughs. "That's cool," he says. "I'll keep the guys off your case."

O. finishes his Gatorade and crushes the bottle in his fist. I do the same. O. burps really loudly, and I burp, too.

"So what's up with that new girl?" O. says.

"Which one?"

"Don't play dumb with me," O. says. "I see you giving her the eye."

"You mean April."

"Pretty hot. She a sophomore like you?"

I start to feel nervous. I don't like talking about this with O.

"There's nothing going on," I say. "I mean, she knows I'm alive, but that's about it."

"Do you want to go out with her?"

O. studies my face. I want to tell him everything. I want to know if he believes in love at second sight or if he thinks it's stupid. Every girl in school is in love with O. He has to know something about this.

O. says, "I'm worried about you losing focus."

"I won't," I say.

"She's just a girl. Keep it in perspective. That's all I'm saying."

"It's in perspective."

O. grabs the ball out of my hands and drops back to pass. "Go long," he says, and points to the edge of the backyard.

I start to run.

"Cut left!" O. screams, and I do.

I'm halfway down the backyard, when I start to think about April. Only now I try to put her in perspective. She's nothing special. She's just a girl. That's what I tell myself. Instantly I feel this tickle in my chest, and next thing I know, my asthma takes hold.

I clutch at my chest, pretending I'm adjusting my shirt, but I'm trying to do the chicken wing thing the doctor taught me that helps to open my lungs. Sometimes I can stop the asthma before it goes too far. I have to breathe and relax and think about good things.

"Now cut right!" O. shouts, but I can't. I can't run anymore. I can't even breathe.

I stop and lean over with my hands on my thighs, panting like a dog. I have an inhaler in my pocket, but I don't want O. to see me use it.

"What's going on?" O. says. He comes over fast.

I try to answer him, but I only wheeze.

"Are you sick? Should I call an ambulance?"

I try to tell him no. I move my hand back and forth to wave him off, but he doesn't get it. He pulls out his phone to dial 911.

I fight in my pocket for the inhaler. I yank it out and suck hard. Twice in a row.

"No phone," I squeak. "I'm okay."

I do my best to stand up. When you have an attack, your body wants to double over, but you need to stretch out and open up. I put my hands on the back of my head and do the chicken wing in front of O.

"Do you need some water or something?" O. says.

I feel the reaction slowing down inside me. I shake my head, give him the "one minute" finger.

"It's asthma, right?" O. says.

"Yeah," I say when I can talk again.

"One of my cousins has it. That's how I know."

"I've had it all my life," I say. "But it's gotten worse over the last six months."

I take slow, even breaths.

"Is that why you don't have your consent form?"

"How do you know about that?" I say.

"I heard Coach asking you about it."

"My mom won't sign it."

O. looks into the distance, his hands on his hips like he's thinking about something.

He says, "What if it happens on the field? The asthma."

"It won't."

"It just did."

"I have my inhaler. I'll just take a puff."

"But what if you can't get to it?" O. says. "What if you're trapped in a pileup or something?"

I feel panic rising inside me. O.'s right. I haven't thought it through. What if some guy bangs into me and the inhaler cracks? What if it slips out of my sock and I lose it? What if—?

My lungs tighten again. I put the inhaler back in my hand just in case.

"I have an idea," O. says. "Do you have an extra one of those doohickeys?"

"The inhalers? Yeah."

"What if you gave me one?"

"Do you have asthma, too?"

"Maybe I could hold one for you. Then if anything happens, you'll have a backup on the field."

I stare at O. "You'd do that for me?"

"That's what you do on a team. You back each other up."

I keep forgetting. I'm on a team now. Suddenly I get this feeling like I'm a little kid. I want to cry, and I'm not even sure why.

"I have an idea about the consent form, too," O. says.

"What's your idea?"

"I say we forge it."

child support.

An hour later I walk into Dad's office with the consent form in my backpack. Dad looks up from his spicy tuna roll, a little surprised. I guess when your sweaty, fat son walks into your office at 6:15 p.m., it's a shock to the system.

"Why are you sweating like that?" Dad says.

"I rode my bike straight from practice," I say.

"Your mother wouldn't give you a ride?"

I have to remember not to bad-mouth Mom. Only say good stuff around Dad. That's the most important thing.

"I didn't even ask her," I say. "I wanted the exercise. I'm an athlete now, Dad."

"I'm getting the sense of that," Dad says.

He takes a box of tissues from the credenza behind him and puts them on the desk. I snag a few to wipe my forehead.

"You want a little dinner? We brought in sushi."

"I'm good," I say, even though I could probably eat four

thousand sushi rolls right now. Line them up at face height and start running with my mouth open.

Dad dips a single piece in soy sauce and pops it into his mouth. I look around his giant office. He'd rather eat dinner alone at his desk than spend an hour with us in the kitchen at home. It doesn't make any sense.

"To what do I owe the surprise visit?" Dad says.

"The form, remember?"

"Of course. The form."

I take the consent form out of my backpack and pass it to Dad. I think O. and I did a pretty good job with it. I'll know in about sixty seconds. Dad puts on his reading glasses and switches into serious mode. "This is a standard PYA," he says. PYA. That's Dad-speak for Protect Your Ass. "Crudely written, but it gets the job done."

Dad looks up at me.

"Are you sure you want to do this?"

"Absolutely."

Dad examines Mom's signature.

"What did your mother say about it?"

"She's a little nervous," I say. I have to keep it realistic or Dad will know something's up.

Dad chuckles. "That's the understatement of the year. She's Chicken Little in a catering apron."

I hate when Dad talks like that. "She might be anxious, but she believes in me," I say.

"We both believe in you, Andy. Don't forget that."

Dad takes an expensive fountain pen out of his desk and puts it next to the form.

"We play eleven games this season. You can come to some, right?" I say.

Dad sighs. "We haven't had a chance to talk, you and I. My date has been moved up."

"What date?"

"My start date. They want me in New York ASAP. November first at the latest."

"That's so soon."

I'm sweating again, and I feel like I can't breathe. It's already September and Dad is leaving November first. That's less than seven weeks away. Seven weeks until our family is destroyed.

"Promise me you won't say anything to your mother or sister. I want to tell them myself."

"I promise," I say.

I feel like I'm in one of those dreams where you're running, but the location keeps changing so you never know where you are.

"Tell me something," Dad says. "How's your mom holding up?"

"She's holding."

"Is there anything I can do?"

What can I say to that? *Come home.* Or maybe, *You never should have left in the first place.* I sit for a long time, thinking about what I should say to Dad. Finally I give up.

"Sign my form," I say.

Dad picks up the pen, signs, and slides it across the desk to me.

"*Mazel tov,*" he says.

I stand up and put the form in my backpack.

"Before I forget . . . ," Dad says. He takes a check out of his desk. "I threw in a little extra this month. Pay your iPhone bill. Whatever. You know."

I look at the check. It's for eight thousand dollars. In the memo line Dad wrote *child support*.

maybe I've changed.

I'm headed out to practice with the guys when I hear Eytan's voice behind me.

"Is it Halloween?" he says really loudly.

A bunch of football players stop and turn around. Eytan's standing in the door, half in and half out of school, like he's not willing to step into the back area with the jocks. It's probably a smart choice. You would not want to piss these guys off.

"I'll take care of that geek," Bison says, and tugs up his arm band.

"He's an old friend," I say.

"Then I'll kick his ass gently," Bison says. "Out of respect to your former life."

"No. I have to talk to him. I'll catch up to you in a second."

Bison shrugs and continues on with the guys.

I walk over to Eytan. I suddenly feel really awkward in

my football uniform. Standing next to Eytan is like the Hulk standing next to a light pole.

"So it's true," Eytan says.

"Who told you?"

"Nancy Yee."

I make a note to cut off all communication with Nancy Yee. That only means six less words per month, but I'm going to make every one count.

"Not that she had to say anything," Eytan says. "You've missed twelve committee meetings. The last guy to do that was Peter Mercurio, and he was cooking meth."

"I'm not cooking meth."

"This is worse. At least with meth we could put you on *Intervention* or something, cry in a circle and tell you we love you. But this—this is like . . . lobotomy time."

"I like football. It's fun."

Eytan holds up his hand. "Give me a second. I threw up a little in my mouth and I have to swallow."

"I thought you'd be happy for me," I say. "I'm doing something different, you know? Breaking the mold."

"Playing football? That's not different. That's surreal. That's SciFi Channel shit. I mean, do you even know how to play football?"

"I'll learn."

"No. Learning is when you toss a football around in the backyard with your dad on Sunday afternoon. You don't learn by playing varsity for Newton. That's the big leagues."

"Well, that's where they put me."

"Doesn't that sound a little strange to you? You've never played in your life and suddenly you're on the team?"

"Coach said I'm a natural."

"A natural water boy maybe," Eytan says.

"Screw you."

"No. Screw you, *dude*. I'm your best friend, and you totally went Philip Morris on me."

"What does that mean?"

"You've been blowing smoke up my ass for three weeks. Now I've got sphincter cancer. What kind of person gives his best friend sphincter cancer?"

"I wanted to tell you," I say. "I kept putting it off, and I don't know—"

Coach blows his whistle.

"I have to get on the field," I say.

Eytan looks out at the guys grunting in formation.

"You really fit in with those guys?"

"That's my team now," I say.

"I don't even know who I'm talking to," Eytan says.

"Maybe I've changed."

Eytan looks out towards the field, then back to the school. "What was wrong with you before?"

I can't answer that.

Eytan doesn't wait. He goes back into school and slams the door hard behind him.

O. jogs over, motioning me towards the field.

"What was that all about?" he says.

"My best friend," I say. "Used to be."

"That sucks."

Half of me wants to go back into the school and find Eytan. Forget all about football.

"You know about the party Friday?" O. says.

"What party?"

"We always do stuff with the cheerleaders. Hang out. Dance. Whatever."

"Nobody told me."

"I'm telling you. You can come, right?"

"Sure," I say.

Coach blows a triple tap on his whistle. If he gets to four, it's bend-over-and-kiss-your-ass-good-bye time.

"Check it out," I say.

I dig in my waistband and pull out the consent form. O. looks at the signature lines.

"Looks like your parents approve," he says.

"They're thrilled," I say. "Their son is a football player."

mom picks, I unpick.

I've got ten shirts laid out across my bed, and none of them are right. Not even remotely. Definitely not for a party.

I'm not sure what party clothes should look like, but I assume if Mom bought the shirt, it can't be right. The problem is Mom buys all my shirts because I refuse to go into a clothing store. Every time I go, it's the same bad news: "Congratulations. You're fatter."

Mom drags me to the store once every six months so she can get my size. Ten minutes of misery and then I'm free. For the six months after that, clothes magically appear in my room. It's like that fairy tale with the cobbler's elves, only my elf specializes in triple-XL polo shirts.

Even I know that's not going to fly at a football party.

I look at the clock. Seven p.m. I've got half an hour before Rodriguez picks me up.

I wish I could call Eytan and ask him what to wear. He knows about stuff like this a lot better than I do. Unfortunately he hates my guts right now. If he saw my number on his cell phone, he'd probably throw it under a bus.

That leaves me with two options. I can pretend I've got food poisoning and miss the party, or I can talk to my sister.

Explosive diarrhea or Jessica. Not an easy choice.

I tap on her door.

"Go away," a voice says.

"You don't even know who it is," I say.

"Now I do. Go away."

I open her door anyway. Desperate times, you know? She's standing in front of the mirror in her bra, pinching the fat under her arms.

Now I'm going to have to stab my eyes out.

"What the hell, Andy!"

"I'm sorry," I say.

She covers herself up with a T-shirt and flops down on the bed. She buries her head under a pillow.

"I'm sorry to bother you," I say, "but I need help. It's serious."

I hear an annoyed groan from under the pillow.

"I'm going to a party," I say.

"I'll call TMZ and let them know."

"A varsity-football party. With cheerleaders."

She sits up and looks at me. "How did you get invited to a football party?"

"I can't tell you," I say.

"Then I can't help you." She sits back on the bed and crosses her arms.

"Listen. You can't tell anyone," I tell her. "You have to promise."

She waits. I look at my watch. 7:10.

"I'm on the team," I say.

"Okay, I just slipped into another dimension for a second and my ears stopped working. Say that again."

"I made the team."

"You made varsity?"

"Yes."

"That's like Ugly Betty winning *America's Next Top Model.*"

I'd love to fling a couple dozen insults back at her, but I keep my mouth shut.

"What about Mom?" Jessica says.

"She doesn't know."

Jessica's eyes narrow. She loves secrets. She's just bad at keeping them.

"What do you want from me?" she says.

"Dress me."

Jessica smiles. "Why didn't you say so?"

She grabs my arm and pulls me into my room. We survey the clothes spread all over my bed.

"What do you think?" I say.

"Jewish-mother chic," Jessica says. "You're doomed."

"Fix it."

"Okay," she says, "this is totally like a *Project Runway* challenge." She bites at her upper lip. "Question: In a perfect world, what do you want to wear?"

"Size thirty-two jeans."

She raises an eyebrow.

"Here's the thing," she says, and chews on the corner of her thumb. "Football players are big, right?"

"Yeah."

"So we don't need to make you look smaller. We just need to make you look good. Big but good. You know what I mean?"

"There's no such thing."

"Think hip-hop. Think Ice Cube. Don't tuck anything in. It's all in the attitude."

Jessica walks across the room like she's tough. She stops in front of me and busts a move.

I stare at her wide-eyed.

"I hope Mom installed a nanny cam, because I'd like to see that moment again," I say.

"Just give it a try," Jessica says.

I imitate her, walking across the room like I'm tough.

"How was that?" I say.

Jessica looks horrified.

"We'll work on it," she says, and she starts grabbing clothes off my bed.

"One other thing," I say. "Do you know how to dance?"

get tipsy.

I'm sitting in front of a beer. It's not the first beer I've ever seen, but it's the first beer I've ever sat across from. And it's definitely the first one waiting for me to drink it. If Mom saw me right now, she'd check me into rehab. Just in case.

There's a bunch of guys, all standing in a circle and watching me. This is a big deal for them. My first sip of beer. They act like it's something important, some rite of passage, and I didn't even know it was coming. At least with my bar mitzvah I had some advance warning.

"Do we have to send you a text?" Cheesy says.

"About what?"

"Beer. In front of you. Smiley face."

"You gonna hit that, or what?" Rodriguez says.

I sniff the beer. It has a strange smell, like sour bread. It makes me nervous. Plus it's kind of illegal because we're all underage. I guess this is what they mean by peer pressure. I've never really had peers before, so I haven't experienced it.

I look at the guys, then reach down and lift the bottle to my lips. The bitter, ice-cold liquid hits my tongue. I cough and spit foam across the table. A *roar* goes up around me and all the girls at the party look over at us.

"Thatta boy," O. says.

"How's it taste?" Cheesy asks.

"Terrible," I say, and the guys laugh. I take another slug.

"You popped your cherry!" Rodriguez says.

The guys pat me on the back one at a time, and they drift back towards the party.

Towards the girls.

There are a lot of girls here. Not Nancy Yee, acne-and-glasses girls who chew the ends of their hair when they get nervous. These are real girls. Pretty girls who know how to wear makeup to make them look even prettier. They know other things, too. At least according to the guys.

I'm wearing an untucked black T-shirt under a button down. I've got on my largest jeans, which are actually a little baggy since I've been working out so much. Jessica pulled out Mom's cuffs and rolled the pants up on the bottom. I feel like a sloppy freak, but when I look around, I fit in perfectly. Big points for Jessica.

"What are you thinking about?" April says.

She's like a friggin' stealth fighter. When I want her, I can't find her, and when I'm not looking, she's sneaking up on my six.

"Just stuff," I say.

"Good stuff or bad stuff?"

"Not sure."

"You smell like beer. Are you shitfaced?"

"No," I say, but truthfully I feel a little tipsy. I didn't drink more than half a beer, but it must have been a strong half.

"You want a beer?" I say. That's what I hear the guys asking the girls.

"Are you kidding? If my dad smells beer on me, my life is over. Seriously. He'll lock me up until I'm twenty-five."

"That's pretty strict."

"Korean dads, you know? He has to protect the family honor."

"If you drink, it will destroy his honor?"

"Kind of."

"What if you talk to a Jewish boy?"

"Executed," she says. Then she smiles.

Now I'm smiling, too.

"But seriously," she says. "A Korean family is different. We're all connected, like a spiderweb or something. One person makes a wrong step, and it vibrates across the web."

April is standing really close to me, talking loudly so we can hear each other over the music. I know I've looked at her about a thousand times, but it feels like I've never really seen her up close. It's easy to look at girls from a distance, but the closer you get, the scarier it becomes.

"You have blue eyes," I say.

"You just noticed?"

"I guess I never saw them before. I didn't know Asians could have blue eyes."

"We can't, usually," she says. She lowers her voice. "They're contacts."

"Why do you need contacts?"

"I don't need them. I want them. They make me look . . . I don't know . . . different."

I look at April's whitened teeth and her blue eyes. All artificial. All beautiful.

I glance down. I can't help myself. The beer is in control of my eyes.

She adjusts her bra. "Those are real," she says. "In case you were wondering."

"I wasn't looking—"

"It's okay," she says. She pinches my arm and smiles. "You're a good guy, you know?"

"I know."

"And modest, too."

The stereo is booming some hip-hop song I don't recognize. The guys on the football team scream the chorus, bopping their heads with the beat. They're scattered everywhere. Bison is on the sofa making out with some girl. O. is in an armchair with Lisa Jacobs sitting on his lap. A bunch of people are dancing. I bop my head like the guys do.

Suddenly I feel good. I'm at a party on a Friday night with April next to me. I'm a guy and I've got a girl, and I'm surrounded by other guys with their girls.

It's like I'm normal.

Even more amazing, I don't feel fat right now. Maybe it's because of the beer. Maybe I'm still fat, only the beer makes me numb so I can't really feel it. When the beer wears off, I'll be enormous again. Or maybe it's something else. With April next to me, at a party with the team, the rules are different. I'm not really fat. I'm big, like Jessica said.

"Do you have a boyfriend?" I say. As soon as I say it, I want to take it back.

"Not anymore," April says. "I mean, I used to. At my old school. Kind of. It's a long story."

"I like stories."

"Another time," she says. She runs her fingers through her hair like a comb. A delicious scent of fruit washes over me. "Do you have a girlfriend?" she says.

"Not anymore," I say, even though I've never had a girlfriend. "It's a long story, too."

"I guess we're both single," April says.

"Are you two about to kiss?" O. says. He comes up and puts his arm around my shoulder.

"Shut up," April says. She sounds like a little girl when she says it.

"Hey, there's nothing wrong with a little lip-on-lip action," O. says. "Provided nobody is sporting a cold sore."

"You are *sooo* gross," April says.

O.'s eyes are glassy. "I'm just messing around," he says to April. "But I noticed your hands were empty."

He offers her a beer.

"No, thanks," April says.

"Hey, it's a party," O. says.

"April doesn't drink," I say.

"I drink," April says defensively.

"Well, which is it?" O. says. "Drinky or no drinky? Not that I give a crap either way."

"Drinky," she says, and she grabs the beer from O. and takes a sip.

I can't believe it. We just had a whole conversation about this, but the O-Effect has completely neutralized it.

"What about your dad?" I say.

"Don't have a hemorrhage. That's why they make breath mints," she says.

"Or better yet . . . ," O. says. He takes out a pack of those Listerine strips that burn when you put them on your tongue. "Lista-rents. Two on the tongue and the 'rents don't know what you've been up to." He passes the pack to April. "With my compliments," he says.

We stand there, nobody saying anything.

April looks at me, then shifts her eyes towards O. When I don't do anything, she gives me an elbow. Suddenly I get that she wants to be introduced.

"Do you know April?" I say.

"We've met a few times," O. says. "But I can't say I really know her."

"Let's do something about that," April says, and she holds out her hand. "April Park, cheerleader extraordinaire."

O. takes her hand. "Cheerleader. Well, that explains the short skirts," O. says.

April giggles.

O. pushes her hand down by her side. "You'd better take this back," he says. "I don't trust myself with it."

"You're a pervert," April says. She laughs way too loud. "Hey, I'm going to run to the ladies' room. You guys stay here, okay?"

"Sorry," O. says. "We're required to make the rounds every fifteen minutes. Spread the love. You know."

O. turns his back, hooks his arm around my neck, and pulls me away from her.

"What are you doing?" I say. "I was talking to her."

"Just walk away, baby boy."

"But she asked us to wait."

"We don't wait. We move, and she follows."

"But it was going well," I say. I'm so pissed right now I want to punch O.

"She'll go to the john, fix up her makeup, then come back in five minutes. But only if you don't look for her."

"That's like playing some kind of game."

"Exactly," O. says. "It's all a game. Your only choice is which one you play. Do you want to play the friend game? Or the hot-guy-I-have-to-chase game?"

"When you put it like that . . . ," I say, and I follow O. to the bar.

"Change of subject," O. says. He grabs himself another beer. "Get this: I nailed the *Huckleberry Finn* quiz."

"Seriously?"

"No kidding. B-plus. Burch practically crapped his Depends."

"That's great," I say.

O. looks upstairs towards the bathrooms.

"Here's the deal," O. says. "You've been working hard. Practicing a lot, helping me out. So I'm going to help you out."

"Help me how?"

O. takes a long slug on the beer. "I'm your genie," he says. "Just make a wish."

"What can I wish for?"

"What do you want?" he says.

"You know."

"Say it."

"April."

O. waves his hand in the air like a crazy magician and hops on one foot. It's so ridiculous it makes me laugh.

"Done," he says.

"Bullshit."

"Seriously. I'm going to take care of you."

I suddenly feel excited. It's like a dream I used to have

where I become president. That's what it feels like to be with O. Like I've been elevated.

O. looks over my shoulder.

"Speaking of which . . . hot Asian at six o'clock."

I start to turn around, but he stops me.

"I'm going to walk away, and you keep looking towards the kitchen like you're thinking about something important. Preferably another girl, hotter than April."

He takes the empty beer bottle away from me and replaces it with his own half-full one. I feel strange drinking the beer that was just in O.'s mouth, but I take a long swallow. It's like we're brothers or something.

I see Lisa Jacobs beckoning to O. from the other room. He pats the center of my chest.

"Lisa needs my lips," he says. "You'll be fine."

He walks away backwards, making the magician motions with his hands again.

I stand there for a second, not knowing what to do. I look towards the kitchen. I try to think of another girl. "Bring the hotness," as Eytan used to say. But instead of the hotness, an image of my mother pops into my head. Probably not what O. had in mind.

"Andy," April says from behind me.

O. was right. She came to me. I turn around slowly, trying not to smile.

"How's it going?" I say.

"We're friends, right?" April says.

"Friends? Um, yeah," I say. I drink the beer and try to channel O. "We are good, good friends. Or we could be. If you play your cards right."

"Why are you acting funny?"

"I don't know. Maybe I'm happy."

"Okay, listen," April says. "I want to tell you something. But you have to promise you won't say anything."

"Don't have a hemorrhage," I say. "I don't kiss and tell."

She grabs my arms and pulls me towards her, all the way in so our faces are practically touching.

"I mean it. You can't say a word to anyone."

"Okay," I say. I'm smiling now, wondering what's about to happen.

April stares at me intensely. Her eyes are huge, her cheeks flushed with excitement.

"What's the big secret?" I say.

"Oh my God," she says. "I have such a crush on O."

the nice/mean/nice theory.

I'm lying in bed looking up at the stars swirling around my ceiling. Dad and I put glow-in-the-dark cutouts up when I was Jessica's age. For some reason I never took them down. Maybe I'm still a little drunk, because when I look up, it feels like I'm flying.

There's a tap at my door and Jessica cracks it open.

"How did it go?" she says.

"You should be asleep."

"How can I sleep when you're at a football party?"

It sounds like something Mom would say.

"How did the clothes work?" Jessica says.

"Fine."

"Just fine?"

"I looked good. You did a good job."

Jessica beams. She comes into the room uninvited and sits on the edge of my bed.

"Did you meet anyone famous?" she says.

"There's no one famous at Newton."

"O. Douglas," Jessica says.

"How do you know about O. Douglas?"

"What do you mean? Everyone knows."

I lie back and groan. I wish my ceiling was really the sky, and I could take off and never come back.

Jessica says, "You smell like beer and Listerine."

"How do you know what beer smells like?"

"From the weddings, stupid."

Jessica lies down next to me. I don't think she's been in my bed since she was five. She used to try and get me to play dolls with her. Sometimes she'd want to sleep with me when she had a bad dream.

"What am I going to do?" I say.

"About what?"

"I have problems," I say. "You wouldn't understand." But as the words leave my mouth, I realize she might actually understand. She's popular. She's got boys chasing her. Even if she's only twelve, she probably knows more about this than I do.

"Jessica, what would you do if you liked a boy, but he didn't like you back?"

"That would never happen," she says.

"Hypothetically."

"What does that mean?"

"Okay, pretend *your friend* likes a guy, but he likes another girl instead. What advice would you give her?"

"I'd tell her to be mean to him."

"Be mean?"

"Sometimes when you're a jerk, guys notice you more. Or wait, it's even better if you're nice, then mean, then nice again. That confuses them."

I can't believe I'm taking advice from a twelve-year-old. But I think about O. telling me to walk away from April. It was kind of the same advice. Maybe Jessica is on to something.

"So what's O. Douglas like?" Jessica says.

"I'll introduce you some time."

"No way!" Jessica says. She gets so excited, she kicks her feet and makes the bed shake.

O. seems to have that effect on people.

Especially girls.

thighs dancing in fluorescent light.

I get to AP History before everyone else. I look around the class. It's hard to know where to sit these days. My old desk next to Eytan is out of the question. The left side in the back is the April zone. The front is Nancy Yee brainiac territory.

I decide to pick the most neutral area. Center of the class, one-third of the way back. Switzerland.

When April comes in, I hold my breath and put a nasty look on my face. I figure I did nice the other night, so it's time for mean. Just like Jessica suggested.

April glances at her regular desk in the back left, but she doesn't sit there. She walks up to me instead.

"Hi, Andy."

"What do you want?" I say. I try to say it like Jessica would, like I'm annoyed by everything in the world, especially if it has a pulse.

April totally misses the point. She touches the chair next to me. "Anyone here?" she says.

"It's free," I say, like I could care less.

I'm thinking she's going to sit down quickly and ask me a question, but she sits and settles, putting her books underneath, wiping off the desk, arranging various thinks like she's decorating a house. For a second I imagine we're married, and she's puttering around our living room moving furniture and watering plants.

Eytan walks in and heads straight for his old desk. He doesn't even look at me or April.

"You and O. seem like friends," April says.

My breakfast does a backflip in my stomach.

"Friends?"

"You're always hanging out together and talking, laughing about things."

"We're helping each other out," I say.

"I don't think he likes me," April says.

"Why do you say that?"

"The party was the first time he's ever talked to me. He usually ignores me. It's like he's got a problem with me, but he won't say it. Or maybe someone else has a problem with me."

She waits for me to say something. I think she's talking about Lisa Jacobs, but I can't be sure.

"Does O. hate me?"

"I don't think so." I try to swallow, but my mouth is completely dry. "Why do you care?" I say.

"He's the captain," she says.

"So?"

"It's important."

"What's important?"

"It's a reputation thing," she says. "If he likes you, your stock goes up."

The door opens and Nancy Yee walks into class. She's wearing a short dress over jeans, and she's got a jacket over the dress, and something like a sweater over the jacket. It looks like she's wearing three different people's clothes at the same time. Jessica would have a coronary.

Nancy doesn't sit at her usual desk. She crosses past April and me and walks to the back of the room. To Eytan.

"What's up, little lady?" I hear him say.

Nancy smiles wide and flips her bangs. Is it my imagination, or has her acne cleared up a little?

"Anyone here?" she says.

"There happens to be an opening," Eytan says, and he brushes off the chair like a maître d'.

Nancy giggles and sits in my old chair.

"Andy!" April sighs, frustrated because I'm not paying attention.

"You said you didn't care about stuff like that," I say.

"Like what?"

"Reputation. Remember that day in the hall? You said you didn't care whether I was a jock or not. That isn't what you're about. That's what you told me."

"I don't care, but it's still important. Not to me, but to the other girls." She looks at me for a long second. "Don't play dumb," she says. "You know your stock has gone way up."

"Has it?"

"Sure. People talk about you now. People who didn't know you existed before."

"You mean because I'm on the team."

"Um . . . yeah," she says, like it's the most obvious thing in the world.

I'm not really playing dumb. I am dumb. What do I know about all this? There are popular kids and unpopular kids, losers and winners, geeks and players. That much I know. But the variations on the theme, whose stock is up and whose is down, the nuances of it all—I've got no idea.

People are coming into the room now, and April is leaning all the way over with her forearm crossed over mine. I can feel our thighs touching under the desk like they're dancing.

April presses the top of my arm. She leans over until her lips are an inch from my ear.

"Will you talk to him for me?" she says.

Be mean. That's what I keep reminding myself.

"Talk to him yourself," I say.

"How can I do that?"

"I'm tutoring him after school. We're meeting at Papa Gino's."

Oops. I was trying to be mean, and I think I just invited April for pizza.

"Oh, I could kiss you!" she says.

I hold my breath, waiting to feel April's lips against my skin—

But it doesn't happen.

Instead she sits back in her chair, opens a notebook, and pops the cap off a Hello Kitty pen.

I hear Eytan laughing behind me. I turn quickly, but he's not laughing at me. He's looking at something Nancy Yee drew in her sketchbook.

I turn back to April. Her smell is all around me, the fruity April scent that I remember from the first time I met her back at the wedding. It's delicious and painful at the same time, like the smell of a fresh-baked pie you know you can't have.

april sucks my straw.

"Dude, you're going through that pizza like a buzz saw," O. says.

I'm halfway through a large extra cheese with hamburger, and O. hasn't even started on his second slice yet. I pick off a big chunk of burger and pop it in my mouth.

"I'm hungry," I say.

"It's cool with me. Keep your weight up. It's a good thing."

"What do you care if I have a heart attack, right? As long as I make the blocks for you."

O. puts his slice down.

"What's up with you today?" he says.

I close my copy of *Huckleberry Finn* and put my Diet Coke on it like it's a coaster.

"You screwed up," I say.

"What are you talking about?"

"At the party the other night. April doesn't have a thing for me. You were wrong."

"But she came right up to you. I saw her. She was all over you."

"She was all over me because she's interested in you," I say.

O. looks at me, wide-eyed.

"But I have a girlfriend," he says.

"Like that matters."

O. is so dense sometimes. He doesn't get that he's a star. For all I know, that's part of being a star. You can pretend you're not one because everyone already knows.

Suddenly April walks by the front window.

"Crap. I messed up and told her we'd be here. I didn't think she'd actually show up."

"April's here?" he says. "Okay, let's nip this in the bud."

April catches my eye. She waves in a goofy, fake-surprised way and comes towards us.

"Wow. What a coincidence," she says. "What are you guys doing here?"

O. sits there silently with his arms crossed.

"Studying," I say.

"That's cool," she says. She looks down at the table. "*Huckleberry Finn*. One of my faves."

"Yeah, it's a good one," I say.

"It's lovely to live on a raft," April says.

A quote from the book. Pretty impressive.

O. motions towards me. "My boy is taking me through it," he says. "He's a genius, this guy."

"I know it," April says.

Silence.

"Well, I don't want to interrupt you guys," April says.

"You want to join us?" I say.

O. shakes his head like I'm nuts.

"Sure!" April says. "But just for a second. I mean, I'm picking up something to go."

I have to give April props. She's an amazing liar.

She sits down between O. and me and adjusts her genius glasses. She's wearing a tight blouse that shows off her cleavage. I've never seen her wear anything like that before. I notice O. glances down.

"Lisa tells me you've been helping her out," O. says.

April says, "Yeah. We're doing Chem together. A lot of people have trouble with it, but it's a cinch for me. I have a science background because of my dad."

"Lisa's not really a science-and-math type," O. says. "But she's good at other things."

He grins like he might have just said something crude.

"Everyone's good at different things," April says. "And if you're not good, you can always learn."

"You just need the right teacher," O. says.

He reaches up and arranges his hair. Which means

he's nervous. Which means I'm in deep shit unless I do something.

Now.

I start talking really fast. "That's what it's like for me on varsity," I say. "At first I didn't think I could do it because of—you know—the immense physical challenges. But the guys rallied around me, and when people believe in you, well, anything is possible. It's like you suspend disbelief and there's a shift in the universe. Something like that."

April and O. stare at me.

"What the hell are you talking about?" O. says.

There's a long, uncomfortable pause at the table. It reminds me of sitting with Dad.

April finally breaks the tension. She says, "Can I have a sip of your DC, Andy?"

She doesn't even wait for an answer, just takes my Diet Coke and drinks from my straw. She looks at O. the whole time.

"Lisa said you guys were having some trouble with Calc."

O. grabs his stomach. "Don't mention Calc. I'll heave up a loaf of French bread." He makes a face like a little kid. "The pain . . . dear God, the pain . . ."

April laughs, and as hard as I try to keep a straight face, I end up laughing, too.

Damn it. I don't want to like O. right now. But when he turns on the charm, it's hard not to.

April says, "Seriously, though. If you have any math questions, I'm happy to help."

O. looks at me. "How are *you* with Calc?"

"I haven't done it yet," I say.

I didn't know April was two years ahead in math. Great.

"I'll give you my number. Just in case," April says.

She whips out a pen and snags a napkin from my side of the table. She passes her number to O.

"That's really decent of you," O. says, and he puts it in his pocket. "Hey, listen. I gotta take a squirt. You kids be good while I'm gone, huh?"

He winks at me, then he gets up slowly and swaggers off towards the bathroom.

As soon as he's gone, April bursts into an excited laugh.

"Oh my God! You really are a genius!" she says.

This time she does kiss me. She reaches all the way across the table, takes my face in both hands, and plants one hard on my lips.

"I love you, I love you, I love you!" she says.

She jumps up from her seat.

"I have to go before he gets back. I didn't even order anything, and he'll totally know I lied. I'll call you later, okay?"

"Okay," I say. Then I realize she doesn't have my number. She never asked for it.

She kisses me again, on the cheek this time, and rushes out the door.

I'm stunned. I reach for a slice of pizza, but I can't even take a bite. I want to smash my fist into it.

O. comes back from the bathroom and sits down.

"Well. That was new and interesting," he says.

"What the hell happened?" I say.

"With what?"

I wave my arms in the air like a magician. "With the friggin' abracadabra? Remember?"

"No worries," O. says. "I'll get some help with math, and I'll put in a word for you at the same time. It's perfect."

"It doesn't feel perfect."

"Trust me," O. says.

He takes a final bite of pizza and tosses the crust back in the box.

"I have to admit, dude. You have good taste. She's actually a cool girl," O. says.

circus material.

When I walk into the house, Jessica is watching *America's Next Top Model*.

"How did it go with the girl?" she asks.

I walk right by her and go into the kitchen.

"That nice/mean/nice thing doesn't work with me," she shouts. Then she turns up the volume.

I hear models giggling. I want to run into the living room and kick the screen, but I can barely move. I've gained a thousand pounds since I left Papa Gino's an hour ago. I can hardly lift my legs when I walk. I'm a circus elephant.

I stamp my way into the kitchen, pretending there are little people under me, and every step takes out five or six of them. People scream as they try to avoid my giant hooves. I tear the door off the refrigerator with my trunk. I am hungry. Elephant is hungry.

Mom is on her weekly shopping excursion. The kitchen is empty. Good news for me. Bad news for the kitchen.

Elephant examines the refrigerator. There is nothing special. Elephant is displeased.

He turns around and looks on the counter.

Bingo. Mom's been experimenting with pie.

According to Mom, Jews don't eat a lot of pie. We eat more cake, but she's out to change that. That's why there are three dozen mini pies cooling in front of me on the counter. They're not really tiny, more like one-third size. Scale models of actual pie. I can guess their flavors from the colored bubbles that have percolated up through the vent holes. I reach for the first one and pull off a small piece of crust.

"Are you angry at me?" Jessica says from the doorway. She says it really sweetly, which only makes me angrier. The nice/mean/nice thing does work. Even on her.

"Get away from me!" I say. And she retreats.

Elephant Andy wants his pie, and I will not be interfered with.

I choose blue.

Blueberry. Still warm. I take a bite.

I choose orange.

I hate oranges, but when I bite down, the flavor is not like oranges. It's more like honey-walnut with an orange essence. Hamantachen pie. Mom has hit one out of the park.

Dark red is apple-rhubarb.

Purple is grape.

Bright red is cherry.

I'm eating too many. The evidence is mounting in front

of me, but I can't stop myself. Whole pies are missing from the tray, and still others have circles punched out of the center where I stuck my massive hoof and licked the results.

Bad Elephant. Hide the evidence. Eat from the back of the cabinet like you usually do. Don't eat where everyone can see it. Be smart.

But Elephant Andy is stupid. To hell with being smart. Smart never helped me.

I rotate from blueberry to apple, back to honey-walnut, over to grape. I put a blueberry and an apple on top of each other and bite into them at the same time. The flavors mix like music in my mouth.

Tears fill my eyes. I'm chewing and crying, and my face is hot. I think about Dad alone in his office while we're here in the house. I think about O. taking April's number even though he knew it was a bad idea. Or maybe he didn't know. Maybe he knew and he didn't care. Maybe April's stock is going up. Maybe if I feed her to O., my stock will go up.

The Physics of Fame. New formulas.

I can't figure any of them out, so I eat.

Elephant. Eats. Everything.

I eat and punch the counter and cry, and maybe Jessica is talking to me and telling me to stop but I can't really hear her and the pies keep disappearing. I'm chewing and getting fatter and fatter—

"Andrew!"

I stop.

Mom is standing in the doorway, her face bright red, plastic grocery bags hooked in both hands. Jessica is behind her with a terrified expression on her face.

I'm covered in pie. There are crumbs on my shirt, on the floor. My fingers are stuck together. I'm fat. I'm an animal. I don't care.

"Oh my God," Mom says. "You're killing yourself."

"I tried to stop him," Jessica says.

"Leave me alone," I say. I know I'll feel ashamed later, but I'm numb to it right now. I'm angry, too, but it's far away, a giant balloon of rage drifting high above me.

"What's going on?" Mom says. "Is something wrong?"

I can tell she cares. I could talk to her if I wanted to. I could tell her everything.

But I don't.

invisible.

There are cheerleaders all around, but they can't see me. They talk in loud voices and laugh.

April is here, too, standing off to the side with two girls I don't know. They whisper to each other, leaning in and looking around to make sure they're not being overheard. Since I'm invisible, I walk over so I can listen in. I know it's probably a bad idea, but I do it anyway.

They're talking smack, just like the guys on the team do.

One girl says, "If you were trapped on an island, and Rodriguez and Cheesy were the only two boys there, who would you have babies with?"

"Cheesy has really nice pecs," the first girl says.

"I love Latin food," the other says. They both giggle.

The first cheerleader turns to April. She says, "If there was a nuclear war, and Andy and O. were the only two men left alive, who would you choose?"

April bites her lip, thinking hard.

"Who do you like better?" the first cheerleader says.

"Who's better looking?" another says.

"Who's hot and who's not?" the first one says.

April opens her mouth to answer—

That's when I wake up.

hit or run.

It's quiet on the third floor. Especially after school when everyone has disappeared. All the excitement and drama is gone, and you get a sense of what school really is.

Just a building.

I'm reaching into my locker when I hear April's voice.

"Guess what?" she says.

Her face looks different. She's wearing more makeup than usual, but there's something else. She's glowing.

"I went to O.'s house last night," she says.

"That's great," I say.

"Don't get any ideas."

"I don't have any ideas."

"We just studied. I'm not easy or anything like that."

"I didn't say you were."

April looks at me closely, checking for a reaction. How am I supposed to react?

"Isn't it amazing?" she says.

"What specifically?"

"That I could like this guy who doesn't even know I'm alive, and within a week I'm sitting on the couch at his house."

I'm thinking how amazing it was when I met April for the first time. I thought I'd never see her again, and then she showed up at school. I honestly thought it was a miracle. Now I'm not so sure. Maybe miracles only seem like miracles at the time, and you don't know what they really are until much later.

"Get this," April says. "He calls me 'Apes' for short. It's like his stupid nickname for me. Stupid and funny at the same time."

"I have to get down to practice," I say.

"Me, too," April says. "I'll walk you."

I slam my locker closed. I pull my shirt out from my stomach.

"You and I aren't so different," April says.

"What do you mean?"

"A few years ago—someone like O.? I wouldn't have had a chance."

"Why not?"

She looks down at the ground. "I didn't always look like this," she says.

"What did you look like?"

"I was . . . pudgy."

My mouth drops open.

"I don't believe it. How did you—?"

"My dad sent me to fat camp," April says.

"Oh my God."

"The summer after eighth grade. I was the only Korean girl at fat camp. They called me the Kimchi Cowgirl. You know how fat kids can be really mean to other fat kids."

"I know." I think of Warner sitting on the ground rolling the dodgeball. I hated him, and he wasn't even doing anything.

"I was beyond miserable," April says. "But I lost weight. And when I started high school in Paramus the next year, I went from being this pudgy geek to being . . . I don't know. Whatever I am now."

"The hot girl," I say.

"More like the hot geek," April says.

"Is that when you did the thing with your teeth?"

"Exactly. And the contacts and everything."

"It was like an Extreme Makeover," I say.

"Sort of. But the thing is, you can change your body, but your head doesn't really change, you know? I still feel like the old me sometimes. Like it all could go away any second."

"I kind of feel the same way about football."

"Like you could lose it all?" April says.

"Overnight."

April steps closer to me. She gets this really serious look on her face.

"I'm glad we met each other, Andy. Really I am."

"Me, too," I say.

"Hey, it's the elephant man," Ugo says.

He's standing at the end of the hall in his greasy, stained sweatshirt. I glance down the hall. There's nobody around except April and me.

"Where'd you get a hot piece of ass like that?" Ugo says.

"Shut up," I say.

"Maybe she's from the Last Wish Foundation. Are you dying of cancer or something?" He makes a voice like a kid who can't breathe: "I just . . . want . . . to touch a booby."

"Come on," April says.

She tugs at my arm. There's a staircase at either end of the hall. We could run to the one closest, and maybe Ugo wouldn't follow. Or maybe he'd use that as an excuse to attack. Anyway, I've tried running before. It didn't work.

So I put April behind me, and I turn in Ugo's direction.

"Your bodyguard's not around to protect you this time," he says.

"What's he talking about?" April says.

"I'll tell you later," I say.

"O. Doug-ass," Ugo says.

He cracks his knuckles and starts towards us.

"I'm serious. Let's go," April says. She's pulling on the back of my shirt, trying to get me to go towards the stairs, but I don't go. I stand still, and I watch as Ugo takes another step towards us.

A crazy thought crosses my mind. Ugo looks like a football

sled. He's the same shape, big and rectangular. He's even the color of a sled, or his sweatshirt is. He's a sled with an ugly head coming out the top of it.

And I know what to do with a football sled.

Run at it.

That's what I do now. I run at Ugo. April is saying something behind me, but I don't hear her. I hear this roaring sound. It begins deep in my chest and pours out of my throat—

"Aarrrgggghhh!"

I duck my head at the last second and aim my right shoulder at Ugo's midsection. I tuck my tongue back like Coach taught me so I don't bite it off.

Ugo's mouth opens in a surprised "Oh—"

And I hit the sled.

The sled holds. For a second I think it's not going to budge, but then it gives way, shifting backwards a fraction of an inch. So I push again, harder. Suddenly the sled buckles and flies backwards, and I go with it, pushing and growling, driving Ugo back until we collide with a wall of lockers.

I hear an *"Oomph!"* as the breath rushes from Ugo's lungs and his body deflates under me—

I immediately back up, toe dancing like I was taught, popping from foot to foot, ready to attack again.

Kids are coming into the hall from downstairs. "Fight, fight!" they shout. That brings even more kids.

Ugo is still slumped down by the lockers. I don't know if he's ever been down before, but from the look on his face, it's a fairly new experience. He's slowly coming out of it, shaking his head and rubbing his eyes.

I thought this was a David and Goliath thing, and I could throw one stone and knock the giant out for good. The bigger they are, the harder they fall, right?

Wrong.

Ugo gets up.

He recovers so fast I'm not ready for it. He just leaps forward and swings.

April screams.

Ugo hits.

It's not like boxing, nothing technical like that. It's more like his fist is a hammer, and I'm a nail, and he's determined to drive me into the wall.

But that's not the biggest surprise. The biggest surprise is that I hit back.

I don't know how to box, so I slap. We stand in the middle of the hall like that, slapping and wrestling, surrounded by people shouting. Suddenly there's an opening, so I rush him again. I duck even lower and closer to the ground, and I hit him with everything I've got.

We fly backwards again, but this time when we hit the lockers, there's an ugly *smack* as his head makes contact with the metal. The fight instantly drains out of him, and he slumps to the ground.

It's quiet in the hallway. People stand and look at us. Total shock.

For a terrible second, I think maybe Ugo's dead. I have this CSI moment, an animation of Ugo's fourth vertebrae snapping. I'm sure I've killed him, and I'm going to jail for a thousand years.

Another second goes by, or maybe it's an hour. I can't be sure.

Then Ugo groans and moves around. His eyes open, and he looks at me.

But he doesn't get up.

The crowd bursts into a cheer. People rush forward to congratulate me. I'm trying to hang on to April, but she gets lost in the mass of bodies.

In one second my whole life changes. I'm not the fat weirdo, a tub of lard, the invisible blob, Jurassic Pork. I'm not even Andrew Zansky, football player, anymore.

I'm the guy who kicked Ugo Agademi's ass.

all that testosterone stuff.

I've seen Warner smile through nearly everything. When Ugo bodychecks him, he smiles. When jocks publicly humiliate him, he plays it off with a grin. When Billy Rodenheiser called him Abs of Flab onstage at an assembly in fifth grade, he laughed along with the whole school. He even smiled in seventh grade when they added swimming to the Phys Ed curriculum, and his bathing suit ripped halfway up the diving-board ladder.

But here's something I've never seen.

I'm walking down the hall the day after the Ugo thing when I pass Warner.

I say, "Hey, Warner," like I always do.

His smile drops away. He doesn't say anything back, only moves to the other side of the hall.

"Warner?" I say.

He puts his head down and speeds up like he didn't hear me.

At first I think I must have imagined it. But as the day continues, I get strange reactions from everyone.

The geeks act like Warner. They either pass me cautiously or stay far away from me. I thought I'd be a hero to them, but I'm more like an unknown quantity, something dangerous they might need to be afraid of.

The powerful kids have an entirely different reaction. They simply nod.

Not just athletes. Socialites. Preps. Even Becky Samuelson, spawn of the superstar.

It's so subtle, you could easily miss it. But if you photographed it with one of those high-speed cameras they use to take pictures of raindrops, you'd see it clear as day—heads bobbing all over the hall, little movements that say, *You are one of us. You have entered the realm of the powerful, and we are going to acknowledge you now.*

That's how it goes.

Geeks and outsiders, the popular and respected.

It's like the whole school has split along some invisible fault line.

Later when I'm on the field running laps before practice, Rodriguez says, "So what's the deal? You're a badass now?"

"Not really," I say.

"Don't screw with him," Cheesy says, "or he will mess you up good."

"I heard the story," Bison says. He bangs his fist against his chest. "Respect, baby."

That's how the football players react to the Ugo thing. As far as they're concerned, I've grown a pair of balls. Balls are good when you're on a football team. Big balls are better. And humungous, King Kong–sized balls?

Excelente.

All except O. I'm on my second lap when he jogs up next to me.

"Is it true?" he says. "You beat up that dude?"

"I didn't really beat him up. More like tackled him."

"The guy who was bothering you a couple weeks ago?"

"That's the one."

"You have to be careful," O. says. "People get expelled for fighting."

"He started it," I say.

"When you're an athlete, they hold you to a higher standard," O. says. "If Coach finds out, you're in big trouble."

"Are you going to tell him?" I say.

"Why would I do that?"

We keep jogging. I notice I can keep up with O. now. It's not easy, but I can breathe when I'm running. Not like before.

"O., what happened that day with Ugo? Why did you save me?"

"No reason," he says.

"We never talked about it."

"Drop it," O. says.

April walks across the field towards us. Players and cheerleaders aren't allowed to mix during practice, so she's kind of taking a risk.

"Hi, guys," she says.

"Hey," I say.

We stand there, the three of us, while the team runs by pretending not to look at us.

"Did you hear what this guy did yesterday?" O. says.

A minute ago he was criticizing me, and now he's acting like he's proud. Abracadabra.

"I was there," April says.

"Really? I didn't hear that part of the story," O. says. He squints at me. "You were busting out your *Heroes* moves?"

"It was scary," April says.

"Ugo's a scary dude," I say.

"I mean you," April says. "You scared me. It freaks me out when guys fight. All that testosterone stuff. I think it's bullshit."

A whistle blows from the girls' field, and April runs off.

"That sucked," I say.

"What are you talking about?" O. says. "It was perfect."

"She hates me now."

"No, she's scared of you. That's much better than liking you. You've got an edge now."

"That doesn't make a lot of sense."

"Girls don't sleep with *like*. They sleep with *edge*."

Coach appears from the back of the school, and O. and I start jogging again.

"We're paving the way," O. says. "When I see her tonight, I'll make sure she's moving in the right direction on this."

My throat clenches.

"You're seeing her tonight?" I say.

O. shrugs. "Math tutoring. I'm an idiot, remember?"

a lot can happen in
a millisecond.

Ugo is dancing with Eytan. At least that's what it looks like.

I turn the corner onto the second floor, and I see them at the end of the hall with their arms around each other, moving back and forth like they're practicing a waltz.

That's what it looks like, but that's not what it is.

It's Ugo kicking Eytan's ass.

I'm not seeing the beginning of it. I'm seeing the end. I know because Eytan's face is red like he's holding back tears. Eytan doesn't cry easily. I've only see him cry once, when Sveta went back to Düsseldorf last year.

When I see Eytan and Ugo now, I freeze, not knowing what to do. Should I scream like a girl? Run to get a teacher? Rush down the hall and get into the middle of it? By the time I get there it will be over. And then what? Another cage match with Ugo?

I got away with it the first time, but what about now? If a teacher sees me, I'm dead meat. I'll get detention. Coach will find out, and I'll be kicked off the team. Then my whole plan is in the toilet. Coach will be pissed, the team will hate me, Mom will freak out, and Dad—

Forget it.

All of that, and I haven't helped Eytan at all.

This all goes through my mind at the same time. All in a millisecond, you know? And the next millisecond—

I turn around.

I'm not turning my back on Eytan. I'm just turning in the direction of class. I can't help him, so why make a big thing about it, right? Anyway, there are people all over the place, so nothing really bad can happen. I can go to class, and I know Eytan will be fine.

That's what I do. I put my head down, and I don't look back.

I rush to history class and sit next to April. I breathe in her fruit scent. It's apple today. Not apple pie, but something more subtle. A bowl of green apples, ripening in the sun.

Eytan walks in ten minutes later. His cheeks are blotchy and he has scratch marks on his neck.

"You're late," Ms. Hartwell says.

"I had an emergency," Eytan says, and he looks right at me. He looks at me like he saw me in the hall upstairs. Like he knows everything.

April's thigh touches mine under the desk.

I'm not a bad person. I'm making choices. I'm putting the team first. That's all it is.

I'm not a bad person.

At least that's what I tell myself.

thinner.

"What's the emergency?" Dad says on the phone. "My secretary said you've been calling nonstop."

I can tell he's irritated. Maybe it's because I've left him eight messages this week to tell him about the game. If he had called me back the first time, I wouldn't have had to call the other seven.

"I have a game against Worcester tomorrow," I say.

"Tomorrow . . . ," Dad says. He sounds concerned.

I look up at the stars on my bedroom ceiling. I remember the day Dad and I put them up. I was too short to reach the ceiling, and Dad had to boost me from the waist so I could stick each one on.

"Can you come?" I say.

"Definitely don't want to miss it," Dad says. "It's just that I'm mid-trial. Anything could happen."

Dad holds his hand over the phone and says something to someone.

"I'm back," he says. "So . . . the game. Will your mom be there?"

"Definitely," I say.

I don't know why I lie about Mom. I want Dad to think she's excited for me. Maybe he'll be excited, too.

"If she's there, then you'll have support," Dad says.

"Oh, yeah," I say.

"In case I get tied up."

"She'll be there for me."

"I have to run now, Andy, but let's stay in touch around this. E-mail me, okay? I'll be there if I can. I promise."

There's silence, neither of us knowing what to say next.

The Dad Gap. That's what I'm going to call it from now on.

"Bye," I say just before the phone cuts off.

I look up and Jessica is standing in the doorway.

I'm about to get angry with her for eavesdropping, when she says, "Dad's a jerk sometimes."

"It's true," I say.

"But what can we do?" Jessica says. She shrugs her shoulders and holds out her arms like an old Jewish man. It's funny and sad at the same time.

"Do you want to come in?" I say.

She walks in and plops down on the floor. I toss her a pillow so she has something to sit on. I imagine it hurts to sit on such a tiny butt.

I look at her in her giant T-shirt. It's not just her butt that looks smaller. It's all of her. It doesn't seem possible that she could have lost any weight. There's nothing for her to lose.

"Is everything okay?" I say. "You look kind of skinny."

Her face turns ugly. I probably sound like Mom, trying to get her to eat. Mom's got a tough job. She has to feed Jessica and starve me at the same time.

"I'm not criticizing you," I say. "I mean, look at me. I'm the size of a school bus."

"You look fine, Andy."

"Maybe on Elephantania."

"What's that?"

"It's the fat planet," I say, and I point to a star on my ceiling.

Jessica looks up. "Is that near FlatChesty-5?"

We both laugh. Then Jessica says, "I guess I haven't been hungry lately. But it's not a problem."

"If it is, will you talk to me?"

"Maybe."

I leave it at that. "Maybe" is better than nothing.

"You never told me about the party," she says. She tucks the pillow under her and stretches out on it.

"I told you it went okay," I say.

"That's boring. I want dirt."

"There's no dirt."

"What happened with the girl?" Jessica says.

"Like five million things. I couldn't even tell you all of them. Anyway, I've got a lot on my mind right now."

"Because of the game tomorrow?"

Damn. She heard me tell Dad. "You can't say anything!"

Jessica's eyes light up. "Can I come?" she says.

"Are you crazy?"

"Why not?"

"Mom's not going to let you go out alone on a Friday night without a major interrogation."

Jessica pouts and punches my pillow. She sticks out her tongue like she does when she's thinking hard.

"How about this?" she says. "We can go together."

"Yeah. Great idea."

"If you take me, you'll have the perfect cover. You can say you're taking me to a game. You don't even have to lie."

"Mom won't believe we're going to a game. She knows we hate sports."

"Then we'll say it's something else."

"Like what?" I say. And then it hits me. "A play."

"What play?" Jessica says.

"*Huckleberry Finn.*"

I look over and Jessica is biting her thumbnail. "I don't know anything about *Huckleberry Finn*," she says.

"But I do."

game face.

"Don't let her out of your sight," Mom says as we pull up to school.

"I promise," I say.

"I mean it. You have to hold her hand every minute."

Jessica reaches over from the backseat and makes a big show of clenching my hand.

"Oh, that's so sweet," Mom says. "I haven't seen you two hold hands like that since you were little kids."

"Don't get sentimental," I say. "We're on a tight schedule."

"Yes, sir," Mom says.

Jessica climbs out of the car. "Love you, Mommy," she says, and bats her eyelashes.

Academy Award material. Jessica might end up being a model after all.

"I wish I was coming with you," Mom says. "I really love the theater. But I have to do this cocktail party."

"Next time," I say.

We both wave and smile as Mom pulls away. As soon as the car turns the corner, Jessica lets go of my hand.

"This is awesome," she says.

A black 4Runner pulls into the rear of the parking lot. I point it out to Jessica.

"You see that?" I say. "That's O. Douglas's truck."

"No way!" she says. "Will you introduce me?"

"Promise to behave yourself?"

"I won't tell him you sleep in pajamas, if that's what you mean."

We wait while O. parks. I figure I'll make a big show of introducing Jessica. Between that and the game, she'll be in my debt forever. I'll never have to watch another episode of *Gossip Girl*.

O. gets out of his truck and stretches. I'm just about to call his name when the passenger door opens . . .

. . . and April gets out.

"Is that his girlfriend?" Jessica says.

we're on the same team.

Our team jogs onto the field, and the crowd goes crazy. That's how it is when you're on a team. You don't have to do anything except show up in a uniform, and people react to you. It's a far stretch from Model UN.

Coach keeps me off the field for the kickoff because I can't run very fast. I sneak over towards the cheerleaders and tap Lisa Jacobs on the shoulder.

"That's my kid sister," I say, and I point to Jessica. "Would you keep an eye on her?"

"No problem," Lisa says.

Sometimes I forget that Lisa is nice. I automatically want to hate her because she's so pretty. It's not really fair of me.

Lisa waves to Jessica, and Jessica's face lights up. Now Jessica knows a cheerleader. I'm going to own the TiVo for the rest of my life.

"Good luck," April says as I walk back towards the team. I

ignore her. If I open my mouth right now, I don't know what's going to come out.

Coach puts me in when we take our first possession. I should be excited, but everything feels bad right now. I keep looking over at April to see if she's looking at O. I look at O. to see if he's looking at April. It's like watching a tennis match, and it makes my neck hurt.

When O. puts his hands on my back, I flinch. I'm so angry, I don't even want him to touch me.

"Easy," he says, and pats my back. He must think I'm nervous.

"Haaaa-eeee!" O. screams, and I snap the ball back a second too late. I feel it crunch against his fingers. He adjusts immediately and snatches it up. He completes a pass to Rodriguez for a quick five yards.

"We're off to a good start," he tells everyone in the huddle.

We set for the next play. This time I snap too far back and miss his hands altogether. He has to scurry after the ball, grabbing it off the ground and converting it into a pass before getting crunched by a couple of linemen.

When we get into the huddle this time, O. is pissed.

"Get your head in the game!" he says.

"It's jitters," Cheesy says. He pats my shoulder like he's burping a baby. "He'll settle down."

But I don't settle. I keep sneaking looks at April when I

should be thinking about football. I try to hear the music in my head again. "True Colors." But it's not there. Only static.

I keep telling myself that it shouldn't bother me. April got out of O.'s truck. So what? It's not like they kissed or anything. But as the game goes on, I feel more and more upset.

We're at fourth and ten when the linebacker from Worcester hits me at an angle, then fakes to his left and scoots past me. He knocks down O. before he can get off the pass. The ball goes spinning across the field, ending up between the legs of a Worcester player who dives on top of it.

A quarter of the crowd stands up and goes insane. The Worcester fans. They're less than popular with the home crowd right now. Only slightly less popular than me.

O. stays down for a couple seconds, just long enough that people start to worry. Even I feel a little panic inside. Maybe he's hurt. Maybe the first game of the season will be his last, and it's all my fault.

It seems to take forever, but O. finally crawls to his knees and stands up, and the crowd bursts into applause. O. limps off the field slowly. As he passes by, he grabs my collar and yanks me along with him. The coach calls a quick time-out.

"What the hell is going on out there?!" Coach says.

"I need a second with my boy," O. says.

"Make it fast," Coach says.

O. pulls me away from everyone. I catch sight of Jessica watching us, fascinated.

"What's going on?" he says.

"Jitters. Like Cheesy said."

"Bullshit. We practiced this. We did it a thousand times. Why are you freaking out?"

O. grabs me by the face mask and pulls my head in towards his.

"You gave her a ride," I say.

"Who?"

"April. I saw her get out of your truck."

"Big deal," O. says. "I was being decent."

"What does Lisa think about that?"

"She's got her own car," he says.

"So she doesn't know."

"Don't threaten me, dude."

"It wasn't a threat," I say.

"We're playing for the same team, remember?" O. says.

"Oh, I remember," I say. "We have each other's backs, right? You, me, and *Apes*."

Silence.

"Maybe I'll give Lisa a ride home," I say. "Just to be decent."

O. smiles. "Well, if your mom has room in her Volvo . . ."

"Screw you," I say.

O. sighs heavily.

"Jesus Christ, Andy, we're in the middle of a game." He points to the white line painted on the field. "You cross that line, life stops. That's how it has to be."

The ref is blowing the whistle now. The crowd is shouting, anxious for us to get started.

I don't move.

O. says, "There's nothing going on between me and April."

More whistles blow.

"Are you angry at me?" O. says.

"Yeah."

He knocks hard on the side of my helmet.

"Use it," he says.

Coach comes charging at us.

"Are you ladies done with your picnic?" he says.

"Ready to play, Coach!" I say.

"We need you on defense," Coach says to me.

Coach warned me that he might put me in. A defensive tackle hurt his ankle last scrimmage, so we're short a man.

I jog onto the field while O. heads for the sideline to rest up for our next possession.

O. is right. Everything else has to go away. If I don't get it together, Dad will never see me win a game. April won't know how special I am. Jessica will think I'm a loser.

I take the line.

I shift my strategy from offense to defense. It's like I'm in an alternate universe. Instead of protecting my quarterback, I'm supposed to destroy the other team's.

I squat and wait for the snap. When their center's hand moves, I hit hard, trying to pierce the line.

Another snap, another hit.

Slam. Snap. Slam.

I glance over to the sideline. I know I shouldn't, but I can't help it. Something draws my attention.

It's O. He's talking to April.

They stand together, away from the other cheerleaders. He's probably reading her the riot act, making sure she knows there's nothing going on between them. He's working his magic for me, just like he said he would.

Worcester snaps, and I press the line. I don't get through, but I try my best.

I look to the sideline again.

O. is still talking to April, only now she's laughing. She doesn't look like someone who's getting let down easy. She looks like she's having fun. O. is relaxed and smiling, his helmet balanced in the crook of his arm.

Worcester snaps. I wrestle with a linebacker. When I hit this time, I use my elbows. I make sharp angles and try to stick them into him. Two or three attempts, and my elbow connects in the space beneath his pads, and he crumbles.

Worcester's quarterback appears in front of me, un-protected.

I can see April and O. over his shoulder. O. has his hand on April's arm.

I charge, crashing into the quarterback with all my might. We go down in a tumble, smacking into the ground with a loud *crunch*.

The ball spins loose. I dive for it. People dive on top of me, scrambling for possession.

The weight of all those people presses down on my back. Suddenly I can't breathe. Guys start punching. The ref can't see what happens in a pile. It's every man for himself.

I start to panic. I can't breathe with so much weight on me. I reach for my inhaler, but I can't move my arms. I struggle to get to my sock, but someone pins my shoulders. He thinks I'm fighting to get the ball, but I'm not.

"Get off," I wheeze.

More guys pile on. A knee crushes my shoulder blade.

"I can't breathe," I say, but nobody hears me.

I feel the familiar clenching in my lungs. I'm sucking air through a straw, unable to get enough oxygen, my heart beating faster and faster.

I'm going to die. That's what my head tells me.

It's probably not true. I mean, people do die from asthma attacks, but it's rare. I'm trying to remember the exact statistics, any little piece of information that might calm me down, but nothing comes. My head is screaming, telling me I'm drowning.

I'm going to die, and O. and April will come to my funeral together then comfort each other in the limo on the way home.

That thought makes my lungs clamp down even tighter.

The weight on top of me suddenly lightens. They're yanking people off the pile above me. One by one guys get up. Finally I'm clear, but I don't move.

I should reach for my inhaler. My arms are free now, but they're heavy as stone.

"Andy!" someone shouts, but the voice is far away.

I hear my breath coming in short pants.

I look up from the corner of my eye. Guys stand around me in a circle looking down. Coach is there, too.

"We need an ambulance!" he says.

Coach leans over and puts two fingers on my neck. He's checking for a pulse. Maybe he thinks I'm having a heart attack.

"Get out of the way!" It's O.'s voice, but it sounds like he's a million miles away.

He appears above me, pushing Coach to the side. He digs in his sock, trying to get at something. I remember April writing her number on the napkin at Papa Gino's. I think O. is going to take it out now and wave it in front of my face.

Do you see this? he'll say. *This is what happens when you trust someone.*

But that's not what he does. When his hand finally comes out of his sock, I see what he was looking for.

My backup inhaler.

He screams something, but I can't hear. Only wind in my ears.

O. leans next to me and cradles my head against his knee. He shakes the inhaler and holds it to my lips.

He puts his head by my ear. "Breathe, Andy," he says.

He presses the inhaler, and I feel the moisture spray uselessly against my lips.

"Take a little breath," he says. "You can do it. One, two, three—"

He sprays, and I try to inhale. Maybe I get a little bit into me.

I see Jessica over his shoulder. She's talking on her cell phone, and she's crying, her face puffy with fear.

"Again," O. says.

I hear a siren in the distance.

"One, two, three—"

I time my breath as he presses. The fist in my chest releases the tiniest bit.

"One more time?" O. asks.

I nod, but just barely, trying to say yes with my eyes.

"One, two, three—"

I suck down the medicine. Almost a full dose this time.

"Make way," Coach shouts. Two paramedics fight through the crowd and kneel down next to O. I see the orange of their med kits out of the corner of my eye.

"He's got asthma," O. tells them.

"How long has he been down?" the paramedic says.

"Four or five minutes," Coach says.

"What's your name?" the other paramedic says to me.

"An—" I say. I can't get out my whole name.

"Andy," O. says.

The paramedic is examining my inhaler. His partner says, "Andy, I'm going to give you a shot of epinephrine. Have you had that before?"

I nod. That's what happened when Mom took me to the emergency room when I was little. I got the shot.

One paramedic puts an oxygen mask on me, while the other one injects epinephrine.

"Just relax," the paramedic says.

He rubs my chest in slow circles, like something a dad would do for a little kid. I gasp, tears welling in my eyes. I think I'm crying, but I don't know why. I gasp again, trying to make up for all the oxygen that's been missing.

"Take slow breaths," the paramedic says.

"You're okay, buddy," O. says.

I'm breathing again. And I can see where I am.

I'm lying in the middle of the field. There are bleachers full of people looking down at me. Football players are scattered around pointing at me. The cheerleaders are in a little huddle to the side. April is there.

Now I'm mortified.

"Oh my God. Andy!" It's Mom's voice.

Mom comes running onto the field, her hair flying in all directions. She's wearing a chef's jacket smeared with something that looks like chocolate sauce. Jessica runs towards her, crying hysterically.

"What are you doing? What's going on here?" Mom is asking a hundred questions at a time. She's jumping up and down, pumping her fists like a maniac. It would be funny if it wasn't so scary.

"Will somebody tell me what's happening!"

Coach Bryson says, "Please calm down, Mrs. Zansky. Your son had an asthma attack during the game, but he's all right now."

"What game?" Mom says.

"The football game."

"My son doesn't play football."

She looks at me lying there in my uniform, an oxygen mask on my face, surrounded by paramedics. Her eyes are darting around like a crazy woman—taking in the field, the fans, the other players.

I close my eyes, hoping that when I open them this will all be a dream. I'll be back on the line with O. behind me, one hand on my back, getting ready to call the snap.

I open my eyes.

Mom has collapsed to the ground. She's sitting with her legs sticking straight out and an oxygen mask pulled over her head. Just like me.

Meet the Zanskys. On oxygen.

April tries to get my attention, but I look down at the ground. There's a spray of white paint across the grass, each blade white as a snowflake. I imagine I'm buried in an avalanche, and they don't find my body for a long, long time.

Maybe they never find it.

That would be better.

mom on a rampage.

Jessica is sitting on a bench outside the principal's office. When she sees me, she bursts into tears and grabs on to me.

"I was so scared," she says.

"I'm fine," I say. "Just a little asthma."

That just makes her clamp down and cry harder.

"Is Mom in there?"

"She's on a rampage," Jessica says. "It would be a good time to move in with Dad."

"Don't think I haven't considered it."

Jessica laughs a little. She wipes tears out of her eyes.

"Do you want me to go in with you?" she says.

"No way," I say. I feel guilty enough as it is. Poor Jessica isn't even in high school, and she's already in the principal's office.

"Sit and relax," I say. "I'll try to make it quick."

The second I walk into the office, I know it's not going to be quick. More like slow and painful. Our principal, Caroline

Whitney-Smith, is sitting with a single white piece of paper in front of her on the desk. Mom and Coach are talking in angry voices. They stop when they see me.

"Are you feeling better?" Caroline Whitney-Smith says.

"Much better," I say.

She won't let students call her Mrs. Smith, or even Mrs. Whitney-Smith, because she says it makes her feel like a stranger. We have to say her whole name every time. She calls it a bonding exercise. I call it neurotic.

"Caroline Whitney-Smith and I have been talking," Mom says.

I stare at the paper on the desk. The consent form.

Caroline Whitney-Smith holds it up. "Why don't you start by explaining this paper?"

"That's not my signature," Mom says.

"How did your mother's signature get here?" Caroline Whitney-Smith says.

"I put it there," I say.

Coach looks at me like I just pissed in his whistle. "You forged it," he says.

"I copied it," I say.

"Semantics," Caroline Whitney-Smith says.

She's right. It's a stupid thing to say. But you say stupid things in that situation. You think you're going to be really cool, but you're not.

For a second I consider bringing O. into it. If I wanted to take him down, this would be a perfect opportunity. But then

I think of him leaning over me pressing the inhaler to my lips, and I can't do it.

"You're right. I forged it," I say.

"I risked everything to give you an opportunity—" Coach says. He suddenly moans, sits back, and rubs his belly. "I'm dying for a Tums," he says. He looks at Caroline Whitney-Smith. "Do you have a Tums?"

"I do not have a Tums," she says.

"I have a Tums," Mom says. She digs in her purse. Mom doesn't go anywhere without the contents of a medicine cabinet in her purse.

Coach says, "I had no idea, Mrs. Zansky. Otherwise I would not have allowed this to happen." PYA mode. Smart.

Mom turns bright red. "What if he died out there?"

I put my face in my hands.

"My husband is an attorney," Mom says. "This will not end here, rest assured."

Caroline Whitney-Smith picks up the consent form.

"Pardon me, Mrs. Zansky, but is this your husband's signature?"

Mom stares at the form, then at me, then back at the form.

"That son of a bitch," she says, and a pack of Tums falls out of her hand and spills onto the floor.

things change.

"How could you not know?" Mom says.

"What do you want from me?" Dad says. "It looks like your signature."

I'm sitting on the couch in the living room watching Mom and Dad fight. Just like the old days.

"You don't know my handwriting after all these years?" Mom says.

"I'm sorry I didn't send it out for expert analysis," Dad says.

"It doesn't require an expert," Mom says, "just a father who pays attention."

"If we're going to play the blame game," Dad says, "I have to point out that I'm the one who knew he was playing football. He felt safe enough to come to me."

"Exactly," Mom says. "You're the irresponsible parent who let your asthmatic son play football."

"I don't see why it's irresponsible to let a boy grow up a little. You can't coddle him forever."

"Look at him," Mom says.

Dad looks at me. They both do.

"Look at his weight," Mom says.

They both look down at my stomach.

"I hate you," I say to Mom.

"Hate me all you want," Mom says. "It's my job to take care of you. That's what a parent does."

"Is this really necessary?" Dad says.

"He needs to hear this."

"He needs to hear that he's fat?" Dad says. "He knows he's fat."

"I'm going to my room," I say.

"That's a good idea," Dad says. "I'm sorry you have to be a part of this, Andy. Your mom and I obviously have a few things to work out."

"Stay there," Mom says to me. She turns to Dad. "This is not your house anymore. You don't call the shots. As difficult as that may be for you to comprehend."

Dad takes a deep breath. I can see him trying not to lose his temper, say something he'll regret later during a settlement negotiation.

"Guys, can I say something, please?" I say.

"No," Mom and Dad say at the same time.

"He shouldn't be playing sports in his condition," Mom says.

"That's not what the doctor said."

"How do you know what the doctor said? In fifteen years you've never gone to an appointment."

I say, "Remember how the allergist said it would be good for me to play sports? He said it would expand my breathing capacity."

He also said we should move to Arizona and I should play a wind instrument, but I don't mention those things. I spent two miserable years taking clarinet lessons, and I've never gotten over it. Fat people should not be forced to play thin instruments. It's a cruel visual joke.

"That allergist was a long time ago," Mom says. "Things change."

"Clearly," Dad says.

"This is not a conversation about asthma," Mom says.

"Exactly," Dad says. "It's about your misplaced anger."

"Since when am I angry?" Mom says.

She says it so angrily, it almost makes me laugh.

Dad doesn't say anything. He goes to the window and looks out through the curtains. The streetlight is on in front of the house, a single pool of light in a black frame.

Dad takes a breath.

"I'm going to New York sooner than planned. Did Andy tell you?"

I hear a gasp from the top of the stairs. Jessica is up there eavesdropping.

"He didn't mention it," Mom says.

Mom looks at me. I can see that I'm going to be spending a lot of time in my room in the weeks to come.

"When?" Mom says. Her voice is soft now.

"November first."

Mom takes a breath. "That's it, then."

"Not entirely. I'll be commuting for a while."

"Still," Mom says. "You're going away."

"Yes."

"I wish you well, Edward."

It gets quiet in the living room. Dad walks slowly to the liquor cabinet where he keeps his scotch. When he opens the door, it's empty inside.

"Where's my Glenlivet?" he says.

"Nobody drinks here," Mom says. "Not anymore."

Dad runs his tongue across the front of his teeth. He looks at me on the sofa.

"What about his form, Elizabeth?"

"Absolutely not. He almost died out there. I will not sign that form under any circumstances."

Dad holds his hands out to me. "I tried," he says.

I look at Mom and Dad standing at opposite ends of the room, their arms crossed.

I tried, too.

twisted.

Ugo is roughing up Warner. It's easy to miss at first because they're standing really close to each other at the end of the hall. If you didn't know they were enemies, you might think they were friends sharing a secret together. Except for the fact that Warner's crying, and Ugo has two fingers clamped on his nipple.

Titty Twister.

I know what that's like. It hurts like hell, but the worst part is not the pain. It's the fact that you can't twist what's not there. Titty Twisters remind you that you have titties, that you're a fat kid who maybe deserves to get twisted.

First Eytan, now Warner.

I can't be sure what this is, but I know what it feels like: Ugo can't get to me, so he's targeting my friends. Or my ex-friends. Whatever. I'm sure there's no difference to him.

The question is, what am I going to do about it? I can keep walking away and spend the semester watching Ugo slaughter the rest of the geeks. Or I can stand up. What would O. do?

"Stop it," I say to Ugo.

"Where's your boyfriend?" he says.

Warner is crying behind him. Ugo lets go of his nipple and pushes his chest, pinning him against a locker.

"The rest of your team," Ugo says. "I don't see them around, either."

I don't say anything.

"Which means you have no protection," he says.

"I don't need protection. Remember?"

"Is that what you think?" Ugo says. He yawns, entirely unconcerned. Not at all like someone who got his ass kicked last week.

That gets my mind going. I beat Ugo once. It's true. But I had the element of surprise on my side. What if I can't do it again? What if I get into real trouble?

Maybe the team comes to back me up. Maybe they don't. Maybe they're pissed at being lied to, and they leave me out here alone. I can't be sure.

Ugo takes a fast step towards me, and I flinch.

A dark grin spreads across his face. Guys like Ugo, they may not be smart with the books, but they're smart in other ways. They're smart with reading people.

And I just gave myself away.

"See you around," Ugo says, and throws me a little salute.

He gives Warner one more nasty tweak on his nipple, then he slogs down the hall, walking slowly and dragging his feet, making sure his work boots squeak against the linoleum so I can hear every step.

just plain Zansky.

I go in the other direction towards AP History class. I walk down the same hall I've been walking down for the last six weeks, but everything feels different.

I try to walk like the old me from freshman year.

Who was I back then?

Smart Andrew. Geek Andrew. Fat Andrew.

I thought I was doing okay in those days. I knew I wasn't cool, but I didn't think I was a loser. At least I never felt like a loser when I was hanging out with Eytan.

Of course back then I didn't know what being a winner felt like.

As I walk, I try to wipe out the memory of everything I've learned and seen in the last month. *Eternal Sunshine* my brain. Go back to the beginning when I was just plain Andrew. No love at second sight. No football parties. No hanging out in O.'s backyard.

I take ten steps, walking just like the old me. I'm hoping it will feel familiar and comfortable, but it doesn't.

It feels like I don't know who I am anymore.

a feeble attempt to recapture the dream.

I jog onto the field in my football uniform, picking up pace as I pass the cheerleaders. April looks up, surprised.

I glance at my watch. It's 3:45 and I'm fifteen minutes late for practice, so I'm really going to have to apologize to Coach.

Coach sees me coming. "Zansky!" he calls. He whistles me over.

The Neck watches silently.

"Did your mother change her mind?" Coach says.

"Not exactly."

"So you don't have the form?"

"Not yet," I say.

Coach grits his teeth. "I can't let you play," he says.

"It's in process, Coach."

"Sorry. They'll put my ass in a wood chipper."

"I'll have it tomorrow."

Coach puts his arm around me. "Don't bullshit a bullshitter, son."

"Can't I just practice for one day?" I say.

He takes a step back and twirls his moustache. His voice gets loud. Coach-mode.

"I want you off this field immediately," he says. "Take some downtime. Hit the books."

The guys are staring. The cheerleaders are staring. I think about the game on Friday, sitting on the field with oxygen strapped on my face, my mom sitting on the field ten feet away with her own oxygen.

"Please, Coach." It comes out like a whimper. Desperate. Pitiful.

O. lowers his head.

"It's out of my hands," Coach says.

He reaches across and grasps my shoulder for a second. Then he turns his back on me.

private practice.

I walk home from school alone. Even though I'm depressed as hell, I jog a little. I figure just because I can't practice with the team doesn't mean I can't practice on my own.

I imagine I'm on the field and I hear the whistle blow. Coach is watching me. April is cheering. O. is depending on me.

I sprint to the corner. Then I walk a tight circle with my hands on my hips—the guys call it sucking wind—then I sprint again. It feels dumb doing it in my street clothes with a backpack on, but that just makes me push harder.

The longer I do it, the more it seems like a great plan. I'll have my own private practice every day. I'll stay in shape until I find a way back onto the field.

I pick a point all the way down the street, and I run there as fast as I can. I'm three quarters of the way when I get a terrible cramp in my ribs, and I have to stop in the middle of the sidewalk and grasp my side in pain.

A BMW slows down by the side of the road. The window goes down, and a lady looks at me.

"Excuse me," she says.

I ignore her, rub my chest.

"Young man?"

"What!" I say, breathless.

"Are you having a heart attack?"

Jesus Christ. A fat kid can't even stop and breathe in the street without someone calling 911.

"Do you need help?" the lady says.

"Leave me alone."

I keep walking, trying to rub the pain out of my side. She drives slowly alongside me, watching me carefully.

"I could drive you to the emergency room," she says.

"Screw you," I say.

That does it. She rolls up the window and pulls away.

the sound of salad.

My head is filled with the sound of Caesar salad. The crunch of croutons between my teeth. Crisp lettuce being destroyed in my mouth. When I start to think about football, I chew louder. I reach for more croutons to drown out the thoughts.

I've had to chew a lot lately to keep up. I've spent a week burying April in pizza toppings and crushing O. with pretzels. When I remember the game, I eat chocolate chip cookie dough ice cream by the tablespoonful. I drown the memories in an avalanche of icy cold cream.

Jessica, Mom, and I sit at the table tonight, chewing in silence. Maybe they've got their own things to drown out. I don't know.

I look at Jessica's plate. There are six lettuce leaves in a pile, and she's wiping dressing off of one. She won't eat it until it's practically bare. Mom is moving salad around on the plate but not really eating. Just making angry scraping sounds.

That's our dinner. Three silent people and one empty chair. Lots of lettuce.

And then the doorbell rings.

Our doorbell never rings. Not at this hour. Not at any hour.

"Are you expecting someone?" Mom says. It sounds like an accusation. Like she's had enough surprises for one year.

"No," I say.

This is the most conversation we've had in seventy-two hours.

"I'll get it!" Jessica says. She'll use any excuse not to eat.

"Be careful," Mom says.

While Mom is distracted by the door, I put a second huge tong of Caesar salad on my plate.

"Mom!" Jessica shouts. Her voice sounds funny, like there's some kind of problem.

Mom gets up and goes to the door. I drop the tongs and use my fingers to pick croutons out of the bowl. Big fat ones.

"Andrew! Come here!" Mom shouts.

What the hell's going on out there?

I walk into the living room and I see—get this—half the football team standing in our doorway. O. is in the front with

Cheesy next to him. April's there, too. So is Lisa Jacobs and some other girls I barely know.

"Are these your friends?" Mom says.

Are they? I'm not sure.

O. says, "We're sorry to bother you at home, Mrs. Zansky, but we were hoping to talk to you and Andy."

"Who are you?" she says.

"We're the football squad," he says.

"Varsity," Cheesy says, as if that makes a difference to Mom.

Mom looks at me strangely, like maybe I planned a surprise attack.

"It's okay with me," I say.

Mom sighs. "Who's hungry?" she says.

I was wrong about it being half the team. Actually, it's the whole team and the entire cheer squad. They're stuffed into our living room now—sitting, standing, leaning, girls sitting cross-legged on the floor. Mom quickly goes into catering mode, whipping out trays of mini egg rolls. She's doling them out defensively like little missiles.

Nobody has said why they're here yet. They're just chewing and thanking Mom. Cheesy tries to pick a mini egg roll off the tray. He's got hands like snow shovels, so he really has to concentrate to take just one.

Jessica's eyes are jumping around in her head. She's got twenty hot guys in her house, and ten beautiful cheerleaders. She goes from flirting with guys to being shy to asking the girls about their hair. She keeps walking past O., trying to get his attention.

I sneak looks at April. I want to be angry with her, but when I see her in my house, it's impossible. My head is angry, but my heart keeps opening up all on its on. It pisses me off that I can't just close it and keep it shut.

Mom runs back to the kitchen for more missiles. I'm wondering how long this is going to go on when O. finally says, "If it's all right with you, Mrs. Zansky, we'll get down to business."

Mom freezes like a trapped animal.

"Of course," she says, and smoothes down her apron.

She looks for a place to sit. Rodriguez jumps out of the armchair and brushes it off for her. Mom hesitates. It's Dad's chair, but Rodriguez wouldn't know that.

"Andrew is a very important part of this team," O. says.

Mom sinks into the chair.

"We know he made a mistake, and he has some health problems, but we'd like to help him if we can."

"I don't understand," Mom says.

"We need him," April says.

"You do?" Mom says.

I feel like I'm going to faint.

O. says, "We're hoping there's some way we could work this out."

Mom looks upset. "Of course I want Andrew to be happy," she says.

What else is she going to say? She's sitting across from a thousand pounds of offensive linemen.

"Andrew's our boy," Rodriguez says. "You should see him out there on the field, Mrs. Z."

"I did see him," Mom says.

In an oxygen mask. But she doesn't say that.

"Things won't be the same without him," April says, and she bats her eyes at Mom. I notice Mom soften a bit.

"Andrew has a serious asthma problem," Mom says.

"Is there medicine he could take?" O. asks.

"There is medicine . . . ," Mom says tentatively. She glances at me. I keep my face neutral. "But football is a dangerous game, isn't it?"

"It's a tough game, there's no question," O. says. "But there's a lot of protective technology that's applied in our gear. Safety comes first. Always."

"And we're a team," Bison says. "We protect each other."

"Yeah!" the guys grunt. It comes out really loud in our living room. O. holds up his hands like he doesn't want things to get out of control.

Mom looks around the room, her eyes flitting nervously from person to person.

"I didn't know Andrew had so many friends," she says. She looks at me proudly. "It's nice for a mother to see."

I try to see what she sees. Thirty people, all here to support her son. That's when I notice it's not the entire team. There's one person missing. The Neck.

"Andrew," Mom says, "do you want to play football?"

The whole team looks at me. It's a really strange moment. Mom never asks me questions directly like this, like I might actually have a choice in the matter. She always decides things for me, then we fight over her decision.

"Andrew?" Mom says.

"Earth to Andy," April says, and everyone laughs. But they do it in a nice way, like we're all in this together.

"Do you want to play?" Mom says.

"Yes," I say.

"Even after what happened?" Mom says.

"More than anything," I say.

The room goes quiet. Cheesy crunches down on an egg roll, and it sounds like thunder.

Everyone's waiting for Mom now.

"Okay, then," Mom says softly. "We'll find a way to make it work."

The team bursts into applause.

I get up fast and go to my room to get the consent form. Before she can change her mind.

the sidewalk, the moon, and april.

The party lasts for an hour after Mom signs the form. Everyone is in a great mood, and Mom keeps the hors d'oeuvres flowing. It feels like we just won a game together, only we did it in my living room.

Eventually things start to break up. People drift out to the driveway. I'm walking outside when I notice O. standing alone looking into the backyard.

"Thanks a lot," I tell him.

He motions back towards everyone in the driveway. "We need you. For real."

"At the game last week," I say. "You saved my life."

"You make it sound like some major deal. I just stuck an inhaler in your mouth."

"It was more than that."

"Maybe. I don't know."

O. squeezes my shoulder briefly, then heads back to the driveway. I watch him as he goes, half of him in shadow, half lit up by our porch light. He seems like a hero in that moment. Even the way he refuses to take credit. It's something a true hero would do.

The players say their good-byes and pack themselves into a few cars. Lisa Jacobs get into the passenger seat of O.'s 4Runner. O. climbs in next to her and fires up the engine.

"Are you coming, April?" one of the cheerleaders says.

I look around, and April's still in the driveway behind me.

"I'm going to walk home," April says. She smiles at me. "I live a few blocks from here."

"I didn't know that," I say.

The cheerleader winks and gets in the car with the other guys. O. drives past us slowly. He doesn't look over, just faces forward like he's concentrating on the road.

April and I stand at the end of my driveway. I look back towards the house and see the living room curtains move. Jessica, of course. Harriet the Spy.

"Will you walk me a little?" April says.

"Sure," I say.

We walk through the neighborhood together. April pulls her sweater around her. It's the time of year when summer is definitely over, but it's not completely fall yet.

"What are you thinking?" April says.

"I'm happy."

"Because your mom signed the form."

"That and other things."

April's lips look soft and wet in the moonlight.

"What's going on between you and O.?" I say.

I didn't plan to say that. It just popped out.

"Nothing," April says.

"You said you liked him."

"Everyone likes him."

"*Like* like. You know what I mean," I say.

"That's over. I mean, he has a girlfriend."

"So you don't like him anymore?"

"Why are you asking so many questions? I feel like I'm being interrogated."

That's what Dad used to say when Mom attacked him.

"Sorry," I say.

"Why are you so interested anyway?" April says.

There's a long pause.

This is the moment. It's time to tell April the truth about how I feel. How I've never met anyone like her. How I knew she was different from the first moment I saw her.

But all I can think is that I probably have Caesar salad stuck in my teeth. I'm going to declare my love with a giant, disgusting chunk of lettuce in my gap. I run my tongue around the inside of my mouth. I can't feel anything, but that's no guarantee. Lettuce is tricky like that.

April says, "I don't want you to get hurt, Andy."

"Why would I get hurt?"

We stop in the middle of the sidewalk. She puts her hand on my arm.

"I'm just worried," she says.

My entire body is tingling. Everything is telling me it's time. *Kiss the girl*, the song says. The song is right. I'm sure of it.

But there's another song. The one in my head. It says, *Fat guys don't get to kiss the girl*. This song comes with a YouTube clip. It's a scene of a big fat kid trying to kiss this little, cute girl. She's sitting at a desk, and he's talking to her. Suddenly he's overcome with passion. He leans in to kiss her, and he loses his balance and ends up knocking both of them over and practically crushing her. The title of the clip is "Elephant in Love." When I last checked, it had three million hits.

"You look like you want to say something," April says.

Three million hits of "Elephant in Love" are playing in fast motion in my head.

Screw it.

I take a deep breath, suck in my stomach, lean in, and kiss April.

I'm not sure if I should aim for the lips or the cheek, so I hedge my bets and go in between. I catch the skin next to her nose, but she adjusts at the last second, and our lips meet.

It turns into a long, slow, soft kiss that completely takes my breath away.

My first.

"Well," she says. "I didn't expect that."

"Was it okay?"

"It was nice. How about for you?"

"Nice," I say.

"Yeah," she says.

I look up at the sky. There are real stars out here. They twinkle and go on forever, not at all like the ones on my bedroom ceiling.

"Thanks for helping me with Mom," I say.

"Oh, no problem," she says.

It's completely dark now, and there's a chill in the air. It's just a little cold, but there's something serious about it, like when your chest hurts just before you get the flu.

"I should get home," April says.

"I'll walk you."

"It's just a few blocks from here. I'll be fine."

"I guess I should get home, too," I say.

April smiles. "Do you have my number?"

"No."

"Why don't I give it to you?"

I pull out the iPhone, and she taps it in.

"You're an amazing person, Andy."

"I know," I say, even though I don't.

April laughs.

"And modest, too," she says.

people standing, person sitting.

The whole school is cheering for us.

It's not really the *whole* school, because pep rallies are voluntary now. They changed the policy five years ago when some parents complained and said it was undemocratic to force kids to cheer, even for their own school. So now kids have a choice. If you don't want to go to the pep rally, you can go to the library. That's what I always did—sat in the library studying with Eytan while the school walls echoed with cheering.

Kind of ironic. The first time I go to a pep rally, I'm in it.

Caroline Whitney-Smith kicks things off. She talks about our rivalry with Brookline, how it goes back for nearly one hundred years. One hundred games, one hundred pep rallies before the games. I don't want to be influenced by such a sappy speech, but it's impossible not to be.

Being on a team. Supporting the school. Tradition.

The stuff we used to laugh about in the library. I'm starting to think maybe it really matters.

By the time Caroline Whitney-Smith finishes her speech, I've entered the Matrix. I'm cheering along with everyone else.

Coach starts to introduce us, one player at a time. It seems like I'm on the sideline forever when I hear him say, "Now I'd like to introduce someone really special. Our new secret weapon, the point of the arrow, three hundred and seven pounds of pure grit and muscle—Andrew 'Big Z' Zansky!"

Cheesy gives me a push, and I run onto the gym floor. I'm absolutely mortified. Coach just said my weight in a microphone in front of eight hundred people. I want to grab the mic back and tell everyone that I've lost a lot of weight during practice. I'm probably 290 now, or maybe even 285. Definitely not 307. No way.

But here's the really crazy thing. The crowd *roars*. More than roars. They *explode*. My name, my size—everything about me gets a cheer. I look behind me and the team is applauding, and the cheerleaders are jumping up and down. When I take my place in the lineup, I wedge my helmet against my hip like I've seen O. do, and all the guys pat me hard on the back.

I'm big, and everyone knows it. Maybe they even like it.

Coach waits for the cheers to die down before he starts to announce the next player. He doesn't even get past the "O." before eight hundred people leap to their feet in unison. It's a prison-riot scene from a movie. I'm sure the windows will shatter.

O. takes a breath as the cheers swell to gargantuan proportions, then he slowly jogs towards me, relaxed and completely unselfconscious, exactly the way he was in the hall that first day when we met. It's as if eight hundred people calling his name doesn't even faze him.

He holds out his fist to me, and we bump knuckles. The crowd totally flips out. I'm caught up in it just like everyone else, a huge idiot smile pasted across my face as I call O.'s name and clap my hands, cheering for my own quarterback. It's the O-Effect in full force.

I look out across the stands where everyone is standing and cheering, and a glint of metal catches my eye. There's a guy sitting in a wheelchair off to the side of the bleachers. He's got a cast going all the way up his leg. At first I think he's one of the Slow Gym kids who maybe wants to feel like a part of the action, but when I look carefully I realize I've never seen him before. While everyone else is cheering, he just stares.

Suddenly our eyes meet. There's a strange expression on his face.

I can't be certain, but I'm pretty sure he hates my guts.

percentages.

The guys are really excited in the locker room after the rally. Rodriguez is describing some girl in the crowd who was giving him the eye.

Coach says, "Can I get your attention, gentlemen?"

People stop talking. There's a creaking sound as the wheelchair guy slowly rolls in.

"*Holt!*" someone shouts, and the guys run over to him, shaking his hand and patting him on the back.

"Who's that?" I ask Cheesy, but he ignores me and joins the group.

"How're you feeling?" O. asks as he gently taps Holt's cast.

"Better every day," Holt says. "Another four and I'll be up walking again. That's what the doctor says."

"Four weeks!" Rodriguez says.

"Months," Holt says.

"Oh," Rodriguez says.

"Hey, I want you to meet someone," O. says. He waves me over.

"This the new guy?" Holt says.

O. nods.

Now that I'm close to him, I can see that Holt's huge. He only looks small because he's sitting in the chair.

"Are you tough?" Holt says with a smirk.

"He's hard-core," Bison says.

"He'd better be," Holt says, and everyone chuckles uncomfortably.

"Hey, Coach," Holt says, "you ready for Everest?"

"More than ready," Coach says.

Holt's face goes slack. He looks up at O. "Sorry I let you down," he says.

"You didn't let me down," O. says.

"I let you all down," Holt tells the team. They grunt, disagreeing with him.

Coach interrupts. "It's time to hit the field," he says. He looks down at Holt. "You want to watch practice? Get a little of the old flavor?"

"Nah," Holt says. "I got things to do."

Coach says, "All right then. Let's motivate, ladies."

The guys bark like Marines and head for the stairs. I check my sock and realize I forgot my backup inhaler. I'm taking the pills now, so I probably won't need it. But I have to keep it with me just in case. That's what the doctor told Mom.

I run over to my locker to get it. When I come back, Holt is still there.

"You know who I am?" he says.

"No."

He grunts. "They didn't tell you, huh? Out of sight, out of mind."

"What happened to you?" I say.

He looks down at his cast. "Broken in three places. More than broken. *Shat-tered.*"

He says the word like it's got extra syllables.

"That sucks," I say.

"Not your fault," he says. "Everest."

There's that name again. The mountain in the Himalayas. I'm thinking maybe Holt went on a climbing expedition and fell. It's not like a lot of high-school kids have climbed Everest, but then again, we're in Newton. There's plenty of money floating around. You get back from winter break, and people have pictures from African safaris and stuff like that.

"I have to get to practice," I say.

"Sure, bud," he says. "Keep your head down out there."

"I will."

I climb the stairs towards the field. At the top, I sneak a glance back down.

Holt is sitting there, not moving, staring at the lockers like he's looking for something that's not there anymore.

* * *

"What's Everest?" I ask O. in the huddle.

"Nothing to worry about," he says.

"He's a friggin' monster," Cheesy says.

"Shut up, Cheesy!" one of the guys says.

"You can handle him," O. says.

"It's a person?" I say.

O. seems upset now. He ignores my question and calls the Trojan Horse.

It's our big sneak play. Pretend to hand the ball to a guy who can run, then hand it to a guy who can't.

Me.

It's a great fake-out. Even our own team gets fooled by it in scrimmages.

That's what happens now. O. fakes the handoff to Bison then drops the ball into my bread basket. An opening appears in the defense right in front of me. So I take it.

I run for all I'm worth. I'd like to score a touchdown against our own guys. That's would feel good. I see the goal line coming up before me. I'm pretty sure I'm home free when someone hits me from behind and I go down hard. I struggle to turn over, and I end up face-to-face with the Neck.

"Get out now," he says.

I'm in shock. He hasn't said more than two words to me the whole year.

"I'm not a quitter," I say.

"You're going to get hurt," he says.

"Screw you. You've been trying to get rid of me from the very beginning."

"You got it wrong," he says.

Coach is blowing the whistle, but the Neck isn't moving. He's lying on top of me, talking to me quietly, three inches from my face.

"Listen to me," he says. "Holt was you last year."

"What happened to him?"

"Everest happened."

Guys are running over and shouting for us to break it up. They think maybe we're fighting. The Neck talks even faster.

"You think you're popular," he says. "You think you're part of the team, but you're not."

I think about the team in my living room the other day. Everyone except the Neck.

"Go to hell," I say. "You don't know what you're talking about."

That's when the guys pull him off me.

I lie on the field, his words bouncing around inside my helmet.

One percent of me doesn't believe a word he said.

The other 99 percent knows it's true.

man meets mountain.

I make it to the school library fifteen minutes before it closes. I jump online to look at archived copies of *The Newtonite*.

I've never really read the newspaper before. Who reads their school newspaper, right? I mean, unless you're in it, then you examine it like it's the Dead Sea Scrolls. I've been in it exactly once, a group photo of the Model UN team going to New York City last year. I made sure I was in the back row peeking out from behind Eytan so my fat wouldn't show. I brought home two copies, one to put on Dad's desk, and one to give to Mom.

I've never taken the paper too seriously, but I take it seriously now.

I read the sports section.

I read about O.'s amazing performance last season. I read a sports column that claims Newton is not an amazing all-around team, but more of a good team with one amazing player. The column says that O. is so good, he's like human steroids. He boosts the performance of everyone who comes in contact with him.

I find another article about O.'s chances of playing college ball, how even in his junior year scouts were looking at him. Division One scouts. That's unusual for Newton.

I follow the team's record last year. Win after win. They add up during the season until it seems all but fated that they will have a perfect record. The perfect season with the perfect quarterback.

Until the Brookline game.

Until Everest.

Junior Injured in Football Game.

That's what the headline says. There's a picture of a bunch of players in a circle watching while paramedics strap Holt onto a stretcher. I look at the numbers on the uniforms. Rodriguez, Cheesy, Bison. And #1—O.

They were all there.

I scan the article. As far as I can tell, Everest was a late transfer from another school. He appeared out of nowhere and changed everything. O., who had never been on the ground before, was sacked eight times that game. Holt, the center, went to the hospital with a shattered leg. O. hurt his shoulder. A couple of other guys got banged up pretty good.

And Newton lost their first game of the season by seventeen points.

The Neck was telling the truth. Holt was me last year.

Suddenly I feel like an idiot. I never asked why the center position was open in the first place. Maybe I assumed somebody had graduated. Maybe I didn't think about it at all. I was so excited to be part of the team, I just went along with it.

I wanted to be popular. That's like a dirty word in my old circles, but it's easy to make fun of something when it's not an option. When you couldn't get it even if you wanted it.

I'm popular now.

I don't care what the Neck says. Eight hundred people applauded for me at a pep rally. They heard my weight and they didn't care. I imagine the faces of the cheering people. They were smiling at me, but I wonder, were they really smiling?

Or were they laughing at me?

I print out the article and put it in my pocket.

enojado.

I walk into homeroom the next day and the class bursts into applause. I guess when the whole school sees you at a pep rally in your football uniform, word gets around. Anyone who didn't know me before knows me now.

What do you do when your homeroom applauds for you? It's weird. I nod and wave like I've seen O. do. I thank a couple people and accept their congratulations. Then I move to my regular seat in the back of the room.

I notice Nancy Yee isn't applauding. She's buried neck deep in a copy of *Infinite Jest*. It looks like she's reading a phone book.

I ignore her and sit down.

Almost.

I'm halfway in my chair when I suddenly get stuck. I push a little harder, thinking maybe I hit it at the wrong angle, but I don't slide in like I normally do. I jam.

I know I've been getting bigger the last few weeks. Coach calls it bulking up.

"You need mass to work the line," he told me. "Eat carbs. And for God's sake, try to enjoy it. Things change when you get older. Believe you me."

So I ate carbs. I enjoyed them, too.

Now my mass is greater than the chair will allow. I'm not getting in, so I reverse direction and manage to extract myself with a loud *pop*.

The Physics of Fat. Lousy timing.

Nancy Yee is looking at me now. She's wearing a frayed denim skirt and a T-shirt with colored threads coming out of it in every direction. Her hair is all shaggy. She looks like a big ball of yarn that was attacked by a cat.

"You actually like sitting in the back row, don't you? Sitting alone and reading."

"I don't want to talk to you," she says. She lifts her hands like she's not interested in fighting with me. I look at her shirt again. I squint my eyes and the threads form into a shape.

Sushi. She's wearing a sushi shirt.

Jesus Christ.

"Have you ever heard of the Gap?" I say.

She doesn't say anything.

"It's where normal people shop. In case you didn't know."

I go to the back of the room. Warner's there, of course. He's been standing back there all semester.

I stand next to him. Now neither of us fit.

I slam my books down on the counter. There's a poster that says, ¿CÓMO ESTÁ USTED? with a lot of pictures of faces with different expressions on them. TRISTE. FELIZ. CONFUDIDO. ENOJADO.

I'm *enojado*.

"Thanks for the other day," Warner says. "With Ugo. You know."

"I didn't do anything."

"You saved me."

"I can't save you," I say. "Nobody can save anybody."

Warner smiles uncomfortably. "What's going on?" he says. "You seem upset."

"You wouldn't understand."

He just looks at me. Doesn't say a word.

"It's football, Warner. I don't expect you to know anything about it."

"I didn't want to play football," he says.

"What do you mean you didn't want to?"

"Coach asked me, and I said no."

"Which coach?"

"You know. Coach Bryson."

"He asked *you* to play football?"

"The first week. He told me they needed a big guy to play center this year. He asked me, like, two or three times, but I said no way."

My mind is spinning. I'm thinking about the Neck, the newspaper article in my pocket. I'm remembering the time I saw Warner coming out of Coach's office at the beginning of the semester.

"It's cool that you're doing it," Warner says. "But you're a lot braver than me. I didn't want to get killed. That Everest guy, you know?"

"You've heard of Everest?" I say.

"Everyone's heard of him."

I'm the biggest idiot in history. This proves it.

Ms. Weston is in the middle of taking roll when I say, "I have no place to sit."

She glances up, nods, and goes back to calling roll.

"I said I have no place to sit, Ms. Weston."

She looks at Warner and me, maybe wondering why she's suddenly got Easter Island in the back of her room.

She says, "Can I ask you to take your seat, Mr. Zansky?"

"I don't fit in my seat," I say really loudly. "I'm too big for that little seat."

The class shifts around uncomfortably.

"I'm sorry," she says. "I didn't know. Maybe we could find another—"

"I don't fit anywhere," I say.

Everyone's looking at me now. Even Warner has backed away.

"I don't fit in this goddam school," I say.

"Watch your language, please," Ms. Weston says.

The bell rings, but nobody moves. The show is too good.

I grab my backpack and sling it around. It knocks a bunch of books off the counter. I stomp towards the door. I don't know why, but I kick my desk on the way out. It crashes into the wall and tips over with a loud *crash*.

april (and other things
I don't want).

History class. April is sitting where she always sits. My table.

"Did you know?" I say.

"Know what?"

She smiles. It usually makes me happy when she smiles. But not today.

"Everest," I say.

Her smile drops away. "He's just some big guy," she says. "Nothing to worry about."

"That's not what I asked, April. Did you know? Before I tried out."

"I knew."

"So all that time you were being nice to me—was that just to keep me on the team?"

"How could you say that?" she says.

I'm putting two and two together in my head. O. saving me in the hall. April flirting with me. Everyone coming to my house. I thought I was making a choice to play football, but I can't be sure now.

April looks at me as if she's really hurt, and for a second I think I'm going to crack. I'm going to apologize for yelling at her, for doubting her in the first place, and then I'm going to sit down and smile and wait for that moment when our thighs bump by mistake under the table. Then I'll spend the rest of the day thinking about it, pretending she's my girlfriend.

Pitiful.

I don't crack.

I don't sit next to her.

I walk all the way to the other side of the room and plop down next to Justin. He looks at me like I'm nuts. He's about to say something, but I grunt, and he keeps his mouth shut.

April stares at me, frustrated. It's not like she can come over and make a big scene in front of Justin and the whole class. That would make her look like a fool, and April wouldn't risk that.

everywhere he goes.

I scan the crowd in the cafeteria. I'm looking for O. I've got a lot on my mind, a lot of questions to ask him.

I see groups moving in packs—the jock pack, the geek pack, the loser pack, the hot girls, the cool girls, the sluts, the gearheads, the rockers, the Goths, the Latin kids, the black kids. Groups. Groups.

I try to remember what this world looked like a few weeks ago. Nobody wanted to know me. The whole room felt dangerous. There was only one place I could sit.

Now people smile and catch my eye. They wave. Guys I've never met before pat me on the back. They say, "Kick ass tomorrow." Cliché stuff like that.

I catch sight of O. in the corner of the room. He moves between groups like a presidential candidate. He doesn't fit anywhere; he fits *everywhere*. He could even go over to the Geeks if he wanted to. He'd sit down with them and the whole group would instantly change. They'd be Geeks Plus or Super Geeks or something.

O. can walk anywhere, anytime. He doesn't have to fit. He moves, and people fit around him.

He turns around now, and our eyes meet. Something troubling crosses his face.

I head right for him, but suddenly Caroline Whitney-Smith appears. She starts talking to him about something, and they head out of the room. He glances over his shoulder before they disappear. He mouths something, but I can't tell what it is. Maybe he says "later." Maybe it's "loser."

The iPhone vibrates in my pocket. When I look down, I see Dad's picture. Dad never calls me. It's always the other way around.

I plug my ear with one finger.

"Listen," Dad says the second I pick up. As if I wouldn't be listening to my own phone. "Good news," he says.

"What?"

"I can make it tonight."

"Make what?"

"The Brookline game. You invited me, remember?"

"That's great, Dad."

I must not sound too enthused, because Dad says, "You're playing, aren't you?"

"Sure."

"So I'll finally have a chance to applaud my son from the stands."

"Absolutely."

"I'm ninety percent sure I'll be there," Dad says. "Maybe even ninety-five."

Dad never commits fully to anything. He always builds in an escape clause. Good lawyering in action.

"I can't wait," I say.

There's a pause and then Dad says, "One other thing I need to talk to you about. It's important."

The bell rings.

"I have to go, Dad."

"Oh, that's right. You're in school, aren't you?"

I glance at my watch. Twelve thirty on Friday. What's Dad thinking?

"Can we do it later?" I say.

"Later," Dad says.

He sounds relieved, like whatever it was, he didn't really want to talk about it in the first place.

cards and letters.

I go to O.'s locker after school. It's not hard to find. There's a big banner hanging above it that says, NEWTS KICK GRASS with a painted picture of the Newton Newt kicking up a piece of turf and making the Brookline players tumble. There are cards taped all over the wall—good-luck cards, congratulations cards, even Valentine's Day cards. It's October. Where the hell do girls get Valentine's Day cards to give O.? Do they buy extras in February and save them all year?

I wait around for a few minutes, but I get this creepy feeling like I'm one of O.'s groupies. So I take off down the hall.

I run into Bison on the stairs. There's no practice because of the game today, so everyone's milling around, not knowing what to do with themselves.

"Have you seen O.?" I say.

"Dude, he's looking for you," Bison says.

"Do you know where he is?"

"I think he's out back. You gettin' geared up?"

"First gear," I say.

"First gear? Shit. Get into overdrive," he says. "We're going to need it."

I go out behind the school. It's weird back here right now. The cheerleaders are off. We're off. The field is silent and empty. A ghost field.

Instead of going back, I head towards the equipment shed. It's our private football domain, one of those state secrets that you don't know exists unless you're supposed to know. Sometimes O. and the guys hang out back there.

As I walk, I take the article about Everest out of my pocket and look at it again. I don't want it to be real. I want to have imagined the whole thing.

I look at the picture.

This same field. Holt on a stretcher. O. looking down at him.

It's real.

I walk around to the back of the shed, and I see that I guessed right. O. is back here making out with Lisa Jacobs. They're really into it, kissing like crazy, her hands moving up and down his back. It's one of those moments when the guys on the team would say, "Get a room."

That's what I say now: "Get a room."

Only it doesn't sound funny when I say it. More like I'm angry.

O. spins around, shocked.

I see who he's been kissing, and it's not his girlfriend.

It's April.

It all happens in slow motion:

April's mouth is moving with no sound coming out. O. is saying, "Um, um, um . . ." I'm standing there with the article in my hand.

O. finally says, "Andy. Let me explain."

That snaps me out of it.

"Nothing to explain," I say.

The article about Everest falls from my hand.

I run.

there's this ringing
in my head.

Everything flies through my mind at a million miles per hour. O. and April. April and O.

O. at the party with his arm around me, giving me advice about her. April and me walking in the neighborhood. O. and Lisa Jacobs bumping hips the first time I saw them. All of them in my house, begging my mom, pretending like they're my good friends.

Why?

Why am I so stupid?

Why for any of it?

The iPhone vibrates in my pocket. I glance at it and see April's name.

I hold the phone while it vibrates. I imagine April holding my hand against her lips and humming. I let her hum until she stops.

The phone buzzes again three minutes later. This time it's O. I press IGNORE.

The two of them call me, one after the other, for the next hour.

I don't turn the phone off. I just keep pressing IGNORE. I want them to know I'm getting their calls.

I'm getting them, but I don't care.

the hole in the middle.

"Are you excited, honey?" Mom says. She's standing in the kitchen cooking mini bagels. Her fingers are spinning dough, twisting and pinching, again and again, so fast they're a blur. She's making enough bagels to fill an oil barrel. Literally.

"Excited about what?" I say.

"The game," she says, like I might have gotten hit in the head and forgotten who I am.

"Really excited," I say.

But I'm not excited. I don't even know what I'm going to do. Not yet.

"Who are all these bagels for?" I say.

"I wanted people to have a healthy snack tonight," Mom says. "Instead of that crap they usually have at games."

How does Mom know what they eat at football games? She's never been to one.

This is not about the game. Mom started cooking after I told her Dad was coming tonight. She didn't say anything, just walked into the kitchen and took out a five-pound bag of flour.

Bagels are Dad's favorite.

"Can I have one?" I say.

"Can you eat before the big game?"

"Carbs give you energy," I say.

"I guess it's okay," she says.

Mom letting me have food? This is a first.

I put one of the bagels on my finger like a ring, and I chew it off. Half makes it to my mouth, and half falls onto the floor.

I think about Mom and Dad at the game tonight. Will they sit next to each other? Will they even speak?

I look at the broken bagel on the floor. Mom's distracted, so I pick it up and pop it in my mouth. Then I grab two more handfuls so I can eat them alone in my bedroom.

dad and his echo.

Mom drops me off in front of school, then she and Jessica go to park the car. Mom wanted to walk in with me, but I told her no. I'm not walking into the big game with my mommy holding my hand. No way.

I'm heading for the athlete's entrance when I hear Dad's voice.

"Hey, boy-o. Wait up a sec."

I feel this burst of excitement inside. Dad came to the game!

I turn around to say hi, and I stop.

There's a woman next to Dad. She's wearing a cute dress with a sweater around her shoulders. For a second I think it might be my sister, but it's not.

It's Miriam, Dad's old paralegal.

"How are you?" Dad says. "Excited, huh?"

I love how Dad asks a question and answers it at the same

time. It's like he's having a conversation all by himself, and he doesn't even need you there.

"You remember Miriam," Dad says.

I grunt. I thought Miriam was long gone by now. Why would Dad bring her to my game?

"Your father is thrilled," Miriam says. "He's very proud of you."

"Thanks," I say.

"And we really want you to visit us when we're in New York."

Dad gives her a look.

"What are you talking about?" I say.

"Miriam is moving to New York with me," Dad says.

"I didn't know."

"That's what I was trying to tell you on the phone this morning."

"But you didn't tell me."

"I tried to call you back," Dad says. "You pressed IGNORE."

"Yeah, I was doing a lot of that today."

There's a weird moment while the three of us stand there looking at each other. The Dad Gap again.

"Are you getting married?" I say.

"Whoa, whoa," Dad says, "let's not get ahead of ourselves."

Miriam looks away uncomfortably.

"I have to get inside," I say.

"Of course, of course," Dad says.

There seems to be an echo tonight. Dad's saying every-thing twice.

"Good luck," Miriam says.

Dad reaches over to hug me, but it feels fake, like he's just putting on a show for Miriam.

"By the way," Dad says, "is your mom coming?"

"She's parking the car," I say. "She and Jessica."

"Good, good," Dad says.

roar (of the crowd).

"NEWTS, NEWTS, NEWTS!"

I'm in the locker room all the way in the basement of the school, but I can still hear the crowd. The energy vibrates through the whole building. Friday night. Game night.

Outside it's excitement. Inside it's all business.

I'm adjusting my pads when O. slides over towards me.

"How you doing?" he says.

"What do you care?"

"You didn't answer my calls."

Before I can say anything, Coach walks through the door wearing a suit. The guys wolf whistle.

"You clean up good, Coach," Cheesy says.

Coach grimaces. "I must have gained a few pounds," he says. "These slacks are like a bad hotel. No ballroom."

"Listen," O. says to me. "We'll talk about this after the game."

"That's convenient," I say.

Coach says, "Let's gather round, gentlemen."

I'm supposed to keep quiet now, join the crowd, be a good player. To hell with that.

"We do this right now," I say to O.

"No, we don't," O. says.

"We do it now, or there won't be an after."

"What does that mean?"

"That means I might not be in the mood to play. Maybe I'm sick of taking your hits."

"What's up?" Rodriguez says. "Are you guys having a lover's spat?"

"Shut up," O. says. He grabs me by the sleeve and pulls me out of the room.

"Where are you guys—?" Coach is saying as we slam through the door into the empty hallway outside the locker room.

"Everyone thinks you're a hot shot," I say, "but I know the truth."

O. pokes his finger into my chest. "What happened to-day—it's not what you think. April was giving me a good-luck kiss, and it got a little heated. No big deal."

"Very big deal," I say. "You know I like her."

"You've got a crush. What do you want me to do about it?"

"It's not a crush. I'm in love!"

O. laughs. "Dude, that's not love. You want to dip your wick."

"Is that what you've been doing? Dipping your wick?"

"I can't control who likes me and who doesn't," O. says.

"That's the problem," I say. "Everyone likes you. Everyone wants to be with you. You've already got everything in the world. Why do you have to take what's mine, too?"

"She's not yours. She's a girl. She makes her own choices."

That stops me. I don't want to hear things like that. I'm afraid they might be true.

"I tried to help you," O. says. "I gave you advice. I told you what to do."

"And meanwhile you were moving in on her."

"It just happened," he says. "It wasn't my plan."

"Just like Everest, right? That just happened, too."

O. is quiet. He looks at the ground.

"You went Philip Morris on me," I say.

"I don't know what that means."

"It means you're a liar."

"You knew what you were getting into," O. says.

"I didn't know."

"You knew what the job was, what the center does. If you didn't know at the beginning, you found out fast."

The door to the locker room opens and Cheesy sticks his head out. O. snaps his fingers, and Cheesy goes back inside quickly.

"You set me up," I say.

"That's what you think?"

"That day with Ugo. Why did you help me?"

"I don't know," O. says.

"It was just a coincidence? You happened to be on the third-floor hallway near my locker the day of tryouts?"

"Yes," O. says. He pauses and cracks his knuckles. "No. The truth is Coach asked me to take a look at you."

"A look?"

"We needed a center, and he saw you knock a bunch of guys down in some soccer game. He said I should check you out."

"See how big I am."

"If that's how you want to think of it, fine. I went to look at you. That part's not a coincidence. But that stuff with Ugo, that just happened."

"You decided to save me?"

"You were in trouble. I thought maybe you needed help."

"I didn't."

It's quiet in the hall now. I stand there with my arms folded, looking at the number on O.'s shirt. Number 1.

"You used me, O. Just like you used April. And my mom. You win everyone over so you can get what you want. That's all you care about."

O. takes a long breath and lets it out.

"Maybe you're right," he says.

We stand like that, both of us in uniforms and pads, all

alone in the middle of the hall. It's funny how the pads make it so you can't feel anything on the outside, but you still feel it all inside.

"Maybe I did use you," O. says. "But what about you?"

"What about me?"

"You used me, too."

"That's ridiculous," I say.

"You got exactly what you wanted from me. From all of us."

"What did I get?"

O. doesn't answer.

I think about the stuff April said. How my stock has gone up since I met O. I think about when I walked into homeroom and everyone applauded.

Then I remember the newspaper article, and it all goes away.

"I have a game to play," O. says. "What are you going to do?"

"I'm going to let you," I say.

And I walk away.

why?

Why would I take the field now? I'm going to get crushed by Everest. If I'm lucky, I'll spend the rest of the year rolling around in a wheelchair with a special key for the handicapped elevator tied to my wrist.

Why?

I walk through the dark halls in my football uniform, wandering, not knowing where I should go. Everyone is outside waiting for me. Mom and Dad, April, the team. They're all expecting me to play. I know the scouts have come to see O. today. I know how important this is for him.

"You think you're popular, but you're not." That's what the Neck said.

If I'm not popular, then what am I?

I turn the corner, and I notice some light glowing at the end of the hall. The Bio lab.

Maybe this is the final chapter. This is how the horror film always ends. I'm going to walk into the lab, and all the geeks will be frozen, hanging up in bags. I deserted them, and this is what happened. There will be one bag left. An empty one. With my name on it.

I open the door slowly.

There are no frozen geeks, only one live one.

Eytan.

He's got his glasses on, the little round ones that make him look like a Jewish John Lennon. There's a frog opened up on the table in front of him. He peers inside the frog, then writes something in his notebook, then peers again. He looks up and sees me standing there in my football uniform, and he doesn't even flinch.

"Hi," he says. Like he was expecting me or something.

It's good to hear his voice. I want to run over and hug him, but I doubt that would go over too well. Especially since he's got a scalpel in his hand.

"Am I a bad person?" I say.

He thinks about that for a second. "Let's just say I returned the Friend of the Year T-shirt I bought you."

I look at the frog pinned to the board, his arms raised above his head like he's surrendering to the authorities.

"I'm really sorry," I say.

"You went BLBC. You're not the first."

"BLBC?"

"Bright Lights, Big City. It's a blues song about how people change when they hit the big-time."

I pull at my football jersey. I suddenly feel stupid wearing it.

"I changed a lot, didn't I?" I say.

"Um, yeah," Eytan says, like it's the most obvious thing in the world. "But I don't blame you completely. It's sexy at the top, right?"

"Maybe it's sexy at the bottom, too."

"What does that mean?"

"You and Nancy Yee."

"I'm not doing Nancy Yee."

"Why not?"

"We're study partners. You don't do your study partner. Anyway, she has other plans. And I'm not the one with yellow fever."

Touché. I sit on one of the Bio tables. Eytan puts down the scalpel.

"Let me ask you a question," he says. "Did you even like Model UN?"

"Of course."

"Really?"

"No."

"So why did you join?"

"You're my friend," I say. "I didn't want you to be angry at me."

"So you spent a year and a summer bullshitting me about Model UN?"

"I guess."

"That's twisted."

"It's not like I hated it. I mean, I'm pretty good at it. And I liked hanging out with you," I say.

"But you were pretending. You're always pretending. You can't make everyone happy, you know."

A roar crescendos outside the school. It vibrates long and low through the corridor.

"Shouldn't you be out there?" Eytan says.

"I'm supposed to be."

"What are you going to do?"

"Play. Not play. I don't know."

"Do you want to know what I think?"

I nod.

"It doesn't matter what you decide. Just do it for yourself."

"I hate when people say that. I don't know what it means."

Eytan shrugs. "I don't really know, either. But I felt required to say it."

I look around the room. There's an invisible man on the teacher's desk. Instead of skin, he's got clear plastic so all his muscles and organs are revealed. I think how it would suck to be him, to walk around with everyone able to see what's going on inside you all the time.

"I've got a question for you," I say.

"Shoot."

"What are you doing dissecting a frog on a Friday night?"

"I was in the mood."

"You didn't come to watch me play, did you?"

"Play what?" Eytan says. And he smiles. It's the first smile I've seen from him in a long time.

because.

I listen to the sound of my cleats clicking on the hall floor. The cheers rise and fall on the field outside, growing louder and louder as I move towards the back of the school.

I stop and lean against a locker.

I think about what O. said a long time ago. Why did I try out? What was the real plan?

It was all about April. April and Dad.

April is a lost cause. I should have known it that day at the party. She got too close to the O. magnet. Nobody gets that close and gets away.

I thought April would get to know me, and the love-at-second-sight stuff would kick in. I could win her over. Maybe I thought my magnet was stronger than O.'s. The Z-Effect.

Now I see that I was kidding myself.

It seems crazy now. I play football and get a girlfriend, and somehow that makes Dad and Mom get back together? They come to games every week and hold hands in the bleachers?

Stupid. Embarrassing.

So what now?

April has a crush on O. Dad's leaving with Miriam. Mom's probably sitting in the stands with her trash bag full of bagels, wanting to hit Dad over the head with them. Jessica is next to her doing leg lifts, thinking I'm a loser again.

Playing football won't change anything. It doesn't really matter.

Only when I think about it, it does matter.

It matters to me.

I've been practicing for months. I knocked down Ugo. I'm different now.

I want to go up against Everest. Not because I have to prove anything to anyone.

I just want to see if I can do it.

take the field.

"What happened to you?" Coach says. "You gave me a heart attack."

"I had some thinking to do," I say.

"How'd that go?"

"Pretty good, I suppose. I'm here."

The stands are packed from top to bottom. Everything is a swirl of colors, cheerleaders going nuts, the crowd shouting their heads off. Brookline on one side, Newton on the other.

Mom and Jessica are sitting together on the Newton side. Dad and Miriam are sitting about ten rows below them.

"I want to tell you something," Coach says. He leans in so nobody else can hear. Three thousand people are watching us, but nobody can hear.

"I recruited you," Coach says. "But it was because I saw something in you."

"You talked to O.," I say.

Coach shrugs that off. "I'm talking to you now. Man to man. Can you handle that?"

"Talk," I say.

"It's true that you're big," Coach says, "and Warner's big, and I needed someone big. *We* needed someone big. But big is just the prerequisite. It's like being tall in basketball. You have to be tall to play. But being tall doesn't make you an athlete. It doesn't mean you're any good at it. You get my point?"

"I think so," I say.

I glance at the Brookline players. They're standing together on the opposite sideline. One of them is taller than the others, almost like he's standing on a box. He's a lot wider, too.

Coach says, "Maybe I was wrong not to tell you about Everest." He clears his throat. "What am I saying? I was completely wrong. Maybe that was a mistake. So shoot me. I wanted to win. "

I nod. Coaches. Dads. All the people you want to be perfect end up being human. It kind of sucks.

Coach says, "If you don't want to play today, I'll understand. I'll be disappointed, and I think the guys will be, too, but I couldn't blame you. Not after everything that's happened."

"Um . . . this is a pretty crappy pep talk, Coach."

"I already gave my pep talk. You missed it."

"How was it?"

"Hey, Rodriguez!" Coach shouts. "How was my pep talk today?"

"Out*standing*, Coach! One of your best," Rodriguez says.

"See?" Coach says.

That cracks me up. Coach laughs, too. The team looks at us like we're crazy.

Coach bites nervously at his lip. "What do you think?"

"I'm playing," I say. "But if you keep talking, I might change my mind."

Coach lets out a long breath. "Thank God," he says. "I thought we were screwed there for a second."

something big,
coming towards me fast.

O. and I stand next to each other before the kickoff.

"You decided to play?" he says.

I nod.

"Don't do me any favors," he says. "I can dance around Everest. I can quick-release. He won't get anywhere near me."

"That's fine."

"I'm saying I don't need you."

"I'm playing anyway."

O. kicks some turf with his cleat. "Good for you," he says.

Four quick downs and we get our first possession. In the huddle, O. calls a standard pass play, but before we can break, Rodriguez puts his hands up to stop everyone.

He places an arm around O.'s shoulder, and the huddle goes quiet.

"Protect our boy," Rodriguez says.

He's talking to everyone, but he's looking right at me.

"*Newton!*" the guys scream, and we clap and break.

I step up to the line, and Everest settles in front of me. I see him up close for the first time. He's not so much a mountain as he is a massive, square thing, like one of Mom's industrial freezers. I catch sight of April over his shoulder. She's screaming something. A few weeks ago I might have imagined she was screaming to me, but now I don't think so.

I feel O.'s hand on the small of my back. "Steady," he says.

He shouts, "Hup, hup, *haa-eee!*"

I snap the ball.

Badly.

My fingers feel like they belong to someone else. I nearly fumble, but I recover at the last second and make a sloppy transfer to O.

I instantly convert my backward energy to forward. There's a *crash* as Everest and I connect for the first time. It's the hardest hit I've ever felt. It's not even right to call it a hit. It's more like a car accident.

Before I know what happened, I'm looking up at the sky. The shadow of Everest passes over me as he moves quickly to crush O.

Instinctively I reach up for his ankle, and even though my hand slides right off, the grab slows him down for a half a second—just enough time for O. to scramble out of the way and complete a five-yard pass.

I try to stand up, but my body doesn't work like it should.

The best I can do is to roll over on all fours like a dog and moan for a few seconds.

I feel arms reach under my shoulders to heft me up.

"You okay?" Cheesy says.

"Let go of me," I say.

He backs off, and I bring myself to a standing position alone. I look at Everest, the sheer size of him. That was only one hit, and we still have a whole game to go.

Jesus Christ.

Everest grunts and gets back into position. I try to look him in the eye, but his face is buried in shadow behind the mask. I glance into the crowd. Mom is up in the stands, her mouth frozen in a frightened "Oh." I feel scared inside. I really want to take a puff off my inhaler, but I refuse to take it out in front of Everest. I won't show weakness. I can't.

The ref hands me the ball, and I get down into a crouch.

It doesn't feel like a crouch. It feels like I'm bowing down in front of Everest, like he's the king, and I'm his vassal.

That makes me angry.

"Get your head in the game," O. says, and pats my back.

That's the hard part about football. Staying in the moment. Maybe it's the hard part about life. Things get tough and you want to be somewhere else.

O. calls the play, and I snap the ball perfectly. I grit my teeth and brace for impact. This time I know what to expect from Everest.

But Everest has something else in mind. Somehow he

rises up, puts two hands flat on my back, and leapfrogs over me, pushing me down like a pancake.

It's a brilliant move. No impact at all. Total physics.

He strong-arms O., knocking him to the ground.

First sack.

That's when I realize who I'm up against. Everest is not just big. He's a true athlete. He's got the Physics of Fat, only he's turned it to his advantage.

I'm overmatched. There's no doubt in my mind.

A smart guy would quit now. Get out before it turns really bad or really embarrassing. But the thing is, I'm curious.

I look at Everest. I want to see who he is, how he's managed to pull off the size thing.

He turns away for a second to adjust his equipment. He cracks his neck and stomps his cleats like a bull scraping earth. That's when I see the back of his shirt. It says: EVERS.

That's his name. Evers. That's where "Everest" comes from.

The thought makes me laugh. Everest is just a guy. A high-school student like me. I'm up against a person, not some force of nature.

It's kind of silly, but it motivates me.

This time when I hike, I spring up fast, pushing up and out like Coach taught me, and I hit Evers full-on, chest to chest, shoulder to shoulder. I hit him and dig in with my cleats. I use my elbows in there, too, just to show him I'm not afraid to get up close and personal.

I push and he pushes back, and for a second I think I might go over backwards again, but I dig in even harder and windmill my arms to shift my center of gravity—

And I hold.

It takes every ounce of strength I have. It seems to last a long time, but I'm sure it's only a second. The whistle blows, and the play is over. I release and walk back slowly, trying to catch my breath.

I held my ground against Evers.

O. grabs my face mask and pulls it close to his.

"Way to play the game," he says.

We stand like that for a second, looking into each other's face masks.

Guys are tapping us on the back, but we don't move.

"Get a room," one of the Brookline guys says.

A whistle blows.

O. signals for us to go without a huddle. He does a quick call, and we hit the line fast.

This time after the snap, I use my height—or my lack of height—to my advantage. Instead of hitting Evers chest to chest, I hit him lower. I aim my shoulder into the space just beneath his ribs. It's like putting the back of a chair beneath a doorknob. No matter how hard you try to push it open, it won't budge.

More physics.

I hit him in that soft place and wedge upwards, and there's an *"Oomph!"* as the air is pushed from his lungs.

He's too good to let it take him down. But it does stop him dead in his tracks.

We don't convert the first down, but that's okay. When Evers walks back to the bench, I notice he has one arm pressed against his belly. I hurt him. Just a little.

We gain two more possessions before the half. We score once, and Brookline scores once to counter us. I'm mostly able to hold my ground against Evers. One time he tries a fancy sidestep. He gets by me and sacks O., but O. isn't hurt.

More importantly, I learn the move, and I don't let it happen again.

i can try.

By the second half, the sun is down and the field lights are on. I notice Eytan sitting in the stands, all the way at the top in the corner. It makes me feel good to see him there. Down below, Mom and Jessica are nervously eating bagels. Below them, Dad is clutching Miriam's hand. The whole crowd looks agitated. We're tied 7–7 with Brookline. Anything could happen.

I move up to the line again.

With the lights on, I can see into Evers's mask. When we lean down towards each other, I look him in the eye.

"Round two," he says.

His voice startles me. It's soft, not like you'd expect from such a big guy. I want to say something back, but you know how it is. You always think of the right thing to say an hour later when you're in the bathroom.

"*Hup, haa-eee!*" O. screams, and I snap the ball. Evers and I collide, our pads grinding against one another.

Second half.

We hit again and again, warriors on the field. It's Evers and me, me and Evers. The rest of the world disappears. I don't hear the shouts anymore. I forget that Dad is watching. I'm not even angry at O.

A question pops into my head.

Who do I want to be?

I want to be someone who hits hard, so I do. I want to be strong, and I am.

The next time I glance up, the game is tied 14–14 with six minutes left to play.

We're in the middle of a long campaign, twelve downs in a row, when Coach calls for a time out.

Guys are sucking down Gator like it's going out of style. Green, red, blue. It doesn't matter anymore. Cheesy even has some private stock of pickle juice he calls his superhero sauce. He offers it to me, but I turn him down. If I'm going to have pickles, I want hamburgers, too.

"How are you holding up?" Coach asks me.

"I'm holding."

"Your asthma?"

"It's okay."

I breathe in and out. I move my limbs one at a time. I'm numb all over, but everything's functioning. There's no specific pain, just a full-body ache covering about 87 percent of me.

The whistle blows. Coach pats the side of my helmet.

I run out with the other players and take my place in front of Evers.

"Round three," I say to him. Not original, but at least I opened my mouth.

We hit each other, separate, and hit.

O. starts up our drive again, doing a hell of a job of moving us inside their forty. That's when Brookline starts to panic. Their coach calls two time-outs in a row. He's trying to destroy our rhythm. He starts yanking players off the line and replacing them with subs.

Evers and I wait together on the field. He looks me up and down.

"What's your name?" he says.

"Andy. What's yours?"

"Eugene," he says.

"No way. Your name is really Eugene?"

"Sucks, huh?"

"Not really. Eugene Evers. E. E.—like the poet E. E. Cummings."

"That's not bad," he says. "I never thought of that."

He reaches out and pats me hard on the arm. I think it's a pat. It feels more like being hit with a sledgehammer.

"You ever read T. S. Eliot?" Evers says.

"Yeah, but I don't love him. I'm more of a Dylan Thomas fan."

"Dylan Thomas died young," Evers says, and he cracks his knuckles like it's a threat.

"Be careful or you're going to join him," I say. And I crack my knuckles, too.

Evers smiles. "You're okay, Andy," he says.

"You're okay, too," I say.

The whistle blows, and I fall back into the huddle with the guys.

"What the hell are you doing?" the Neck says. "You were fraternizing out there."

The guys look at me suspiciously.

"How do you know Everest?" Rodriguez says.

"I don't," I say. "We were talking postwar poets."

O. stares at me. Maybe he's wondering if I'm setting him up. I play hard all game, then I let him get crushed in the final minutes. It would be a brilliant strategy.

Bison throws me a dirty look. "I don't know if we can trust you. A guy who disappears before the game."

"Drop it," O. says.

"But, O.—" Bison says.

"We're doing the Trojan Horse," O. says.

"Bad idea," Bison says.

"It's not your call," O. says.

"Are you sure?" Rodriguez says.

The Trojan Horse. My play, the fake-out. O. is going to hand off to me.

If he hands off to me, I'll have to run. If I run, I won't be in front of him anymore.

Evers will.

O. looks at me. "Can you do it?"

"I can try."

"Then try. Break!" O. shouts, and everyone rolls out of the huddle.

O. makes a big show of whispering in Bison's ear. It's what Coach calls Psy-Ops. Psychological Operation. O.'s telegraphing the handoff to Brookline. Telegraphing it in the wrong direction.

I get up to the line, position myself opposite Everest. A running play. My hands are shaking. I can't do it. I'm going to get killed. I'll make a fool out of myself.

That's when I think of the song. "True Colors."

Everest snorts.

I listen to the song in my head.

I feel O.'s touch, pulling me back to the moment.

"Haa-eee!" he shouts, and I press the ball into his hands.

I hit Everest hard and at an angle, but instead of continuing to drive forward, I use the collision to spin me around backwards towards O. It's an elegant move. Like dancing.

I feel Everest hesitate for a second, surprised that I'm not up in his face. I twist around and cup my arms.

O. fakes towards Bison, then shifts back and pops the ball hard into my stomach.

I pivot off to the left, trying to hide the ball in the center of my gut. Out of the corner of my eye I see Everest headed directly for O., but it's not my job to protect him this time. Instead I push off and run as fast as I can towards the goal line. I hear a *crash* behind me as O. gets splattered. But I don't look back.

A couple of Brookline players notice me go. I hope they think I'm confused, or maybe I saw a hot dog on the sideline that I couldn't resist. They can think whatever they like, because I know what I have.

The ball.

By the time they catch on to what's really happening, I'm past them, running for all I'm worth. Unfortunately, all I'm worth is about fifteen yards. That's when I get winded and slow down.

The Brookline defensemen easily catch up to me. I don't get the touchdown. I get massacred.

Whatever.

The important thing is that I make it inside the twenty-yard line before they wrestle me to the ground. That's field-goal range. And Cheesy is known to kick a hell of a field goal.

He kicks one now.

We win. 17–14.

the glow of nothing special.

There's chaos on the field. We shake hands with the Brookline guys, and they quickly retreat as the stands empty and we're mobbed by fans. The last thing I see is Everest looking back at me, giving me the nod. I gesture with my hand like I'm tipping my hat to him.

Coach gets a barrel of Gator poured over his head. It's the only time I've seen his moustache droop. It looks like there's a wet mouse sleeping on his lip.

O. gets hefted on top of the guys' shoulders. I watch him up there, his eyes twinkling. He lives for this stuff. Not just winning. Football. I knew it from the first practice when I saw him on the field. It reminded me of Mom when she's in the kitchen. Or Dad in his office. They're perfectly in their element.

The field is O.'s element. He may get to play college ball or he may not. But he's home now. All the guys are. I can feel it.

Suddenly I'm sad because I know I'm not like them. I

practiced with them. We played together, and I held my own. Tonight we'll celebrate together.

But I don't love this game. Not the way they do. Which brings up an interesting question. If not football, then what do I love?

Dad appears out of the crowd. He runs towards me, smiling and calling my name.

"That was fantastic!" Dad says. "I couldn't believe it was you out there. It's like I had another son and nobody told me."

"It was okay," I say. "I didn't score."

"It was more than okay," Dad says. "Outstanding."

Coach comes over, wringing green liquid out of his shirt. He's smiling, too.

Dad thrusts his hand out towards Coach. "I'm the father," he says.

"Pleasure to meet you," Coach says. "Hell of a game, wasn't it?"

"I was just saying as much to Andrew," Dad says.

Coach puts his arm around my shoulder. "I've got big plans for your boy, Mr. Zansky."

"Do you hear that, Andrew?" Dad says.

"Big plans. We've got ourselves a natural talent here. A diamond in the rough, so to speak."

"You've got three years to polish it," Dad says.

"A little guidance, some strength training. This is just the beginning."

Dad looks so proud, and Coach is really excited. I can see

he's thinking about winning, not just this year, but next year when O. is gone. That makes it hard to say what I have to say, but I take a deep breath, and I do it anyway.

"No thanks, Coach. I quit," I say.

"Quit what?" Coach says.

"Football."

Dad laughs. "You're joking, right?" He nails Coach in the ribs with his elbow.

"I never really liked football. I only did it to impress a girl."

Dad looks at me like I'm crazy. "What's wrong with that?" he says. "That's how I met your mother."

Coach nods like it's a fact of life.

"If I'm going to impress someone," I say, "I'd rather impress them doing something I like."

"But you're good at this," Dad says. He sounds desperate. I know Dad wants me to succeed. Maybe he thinks this is my one chance.

Do you only get one chance? I hope not.

"I'm good at a lot of things," I say.

"Not like this," Dad says.

I think about that for a second. Dad's right. There aren't a lot of things that three thousand people watch you do in a stadium. I imagine taking the American History AP exam in the middle of the field with people watching. I bubble with a number-two pencil and the fans go wild. Never going to happen. Then I imagine writing a short story. That's something else I want to do. But people don't jump up and down when you write a story.

"Take some time to think about things," Coach says.

"I've had lots of time."

Coach twirls his droopy moustache. "Take some more. You don't want to do anything you're going to regret."

A bunch of guys rush past, and they grab Coach and pull him along with them.

"I'm serious," Coach calls back to me. "This team is championship material."

I turn back to Dad. He just stares at me.

"You're quitting?" Dad says. "Why would you say something like that?"

"I don't know."

"I think you do."

"You wouldn't understand, Dad."

"Try me."

You can't out-argue a lawyer. I forget that sometimes.

"It's like I did everything for the wrong reasons," I say.

I think Dad is going to yell at me, but instead he says: "Right and wrong. It gets confusing sometimes, doesn't it?"

"Yeah."

"You think it gets easier when you're older, but it doesn't."

Dad shuffles uncomfortably and kicks the turf with his loafer.

"I don't want you to go to New York," I say.

As soon as I say it, I wish I hadn't. Even though it's what I've been thinking for months. Even though it's the truth.

"You don't just give up an opportunity like this, Andy. They don't come around every day."

I'm not sure if Dad is talking about his new job or football. Before I can ask him, Miriam comes walking towards us across the field.

"Sorry. I had to run to the little girls' room."

"She has a tiny bladder," Dad says. "It's like living with a gerbil."

"Stop that," Miriam says. "It's your son's big day."

"Exactly why you should hold it until we get back to the apartment."

I clear my throat. "Mom's giving me a ride home."

"Okay, then," Dad says. "You'll come by the apartment before we leave?"

"Absolutely," I say.

He musses the top of my hair like he used to do when I was a kid. Then he gives me a hug.

It starts out like the usual Dad hug—more symbolic than anything else—but then he doesn't let go. Neither do I.

"Whatever you decide, you did a good job today. You should be proud," Dad says.

"I am," I say.

I walk away towards the parking lot. When I glance back, the two of them are still there, watching me. Miriam has her arm hooked in Dad's, and they're both waving and smiling.

Maybe it's mean of me, but I don't wave back.

the long short ride home.

"What's O. Douglas really like?" Jessica asks from the front
seat. This is her ten thousandth question about the game, and
it's only a fifteen-minute ride home. I feel a little embarrassed
for her, the way she's so obviously obsessed with the popular
crowd. Who's hot, who's not, et cetera.

All the same stuff that I was obsessed with.

So I don't get angry with her like I usually do. I answer her
questions as best I can. I try to tell her the truth, share my
experience of it all.

I tell her about the time I was playing in O.'s backyard, and
I had an asthma attack. I tell her about my secret deal with
O. about my inhaler. I tell her how I had a crush on April,
how we talked at the party, and I thought she was going to be
my girlfriend. I talk about my theory of love at second sight.
I know Mom's listening, so I leave out the stuff about the
alcohol at the party. But I tell most everything else.

Mom and Jess seem really interested, even during the boring parts. They sigh and gasp, ask a lot more questions.

A funny thing starts to happen.

The more I tell the story, the more it stops feeling like something that happened to someone else, and starts feeling like it happened to me.

When I finish, Mom says, "What an amazing story. You should write some of this down."

"Maybe I will," I say.

Mom turns the corner onto Boylston Street.

"I saw you talking to your father," Mom says.

I think she might get angry, but she doesn't. She just says, "It was nice of him to come to your game."

"I think so, too," I say.

"And bring his friend—" Mom doesn't even finish the sentence before she starts to cry. She takes the corner too fast as she digs in her purse for a tissue. Mom's driving is never great, but when she's driving and crying, I get concerned for our lives.

"I'm so sorry," she says. "It's all a little too much sometimes."

"It's going to be okay, Mom," Jessica says.

Mom sniffles. "It's *my* job to say that."

Mom shoots through a stop sign. Jessica and I trade worried looks.

"Maybe we should go to Papa Gino's," I say, because it's

right down the street, and if I'm going to die, I'd like to do it in the vicinity of pizza.

"I think that's a good idea," Mom says.

We pull into the parking lot, and a few minutes later we're sitting with a large sausage and pepperoni in front of us. We also get a big salad on the side, but it's mostly for show. We put some on our plates, then we concentrate on the pizza. Even Jessica has a slice.

"The sausage is delicious," Mom says.

"Definitely," I say.

Mom put us on the Kosher Diet last year, but it didn't last long. We both realized we liked pork too much to commit.

After a while, Mom starts to tell us a story about her own high-school days. She tells us how she got a crush on a boy and how he didn't like her back. She talks about another boy who liked her too much, and she didn't like him back.

"How did you meet Dad?" Jessica says.

I try to kick her under the table to shut her up, but I don't get to her in time. I'm waiting for Mom to freak out, but she just gets quiet for a minute, and then she starts to talk.

She tells us about the first time she saw Dad playing baseball in college, how good he looked on the field, and how she had to work really hard to get his attention. "All the girls wanted a piece of him," Mom says, "but they couldn't cook like I could. One night I made him a lasagna and brought it to his house after the game with fresh pecorino cheese and a grater. I think the pecorino sealed the deal."

"You can get a lot of mileage with a good cheese," I say.

We sit in Papa Gino's—just the three of us—eating pizza, telling stories, and laughing a little, almost like the old days. I eat four pieces of pizza. I'm about to reach for five when Mom gives me the eye, and I have to stop.

I know we have problems, but tonight they don't bother me so much. I don't know why it is, but everything feels better when I'm eating. I guess I'm just built that way.

expansion.

Eytan and I are walking to AP History together. I'm looking around the school, thinking about all the different things I've done since the beginning of the year.

"What's on your mind?" Eytan says.

"The whole world," I say.

"That's a lot."

"No kidding. My head's killing me."

"Maybe you could think about half the world at a time. Like Monday, Wednesday, Friday you do Western Hemisphere, and Tuesday, Thursday, Saturday you do Eastern."

"What about Sunday?"

"Sunday is for sex. Twenty-four hours of the most depraved and perverse sexual fantasies."

I laugh and punch Eytan in the arm.

"Careful. You've got serious guns now," he says.

I make a muscle and Eytan squeezes it.

"Geez," he says. "You should start wearing T-shirts. Show those babies off a little bit."

"I don't like T-shirts."

"Forget what you like. Do it for me. We could use a few more ladies in our social circle. That's not to say you're not excellent company. But for the purpose of expanding our horizons—"

"It's important to expand," I say.

"I cannot disagree with you," Eytan says.

"But you'll have to do it without my T-shirts."

A couple of cute girls pass us, and they look our way. One of them, a redhead, even smiles.

"Have a beautiful day, ladies," Eytan calls after them.

They giggle as they go down the hall.

Eytan looks at me, one eyebrow raised. "Expansion," he says.

"In your pants, maybe."

He smiles, then his face suddenly gets serious. "Quick question," he says.

"Hit me."

"With all this football stuff—the parties, the practices, the new friends, the cheerleaders, all of it—"

"What's the question?" I say.

"Did you get any?"

"No."

"Son of a bitch."

football players only.

I'm waiting outside the locker room after school. It feels strange to be in the hall without going in. A bunch of the guys pass by in a group.

"What's up, badass?" Rodriguez says. We bump fists.

"Not much," I say.

"You miss us, don't you?"

"Not at all," I say.

"Bullshit," Cheesy says. "It's tough to shower alone. Admit it."

"It's true," I say. Then I pause. "So it doesn't count if my mom is in there with me?"

"Holy crap," Rodriguez says. "You did not just say that."

The guys bust out laughing. Cheesy starts to choke, and they have to slap him on the back. We're all there—Rodriguez, Cheesy, Bison, even the Neck. It's like we're on the line again, just for a second.

"You maybe change your mind about us?" Bison says.

"No," I say.

"Why not? Is there something wrong with us? I mean, other than Cheesy's BO," Bison says.

"It's not you guys. It's just—I have other things I want to do."

"That's friggin' lame," Bison says.

"Easy," Rodriguez says.

"No, I'm serious. We schooled the boy, and he turns around and screws us."

Bison flings open the locker-room door. He stops and looks back at me. "So I'll tell you what, dude. You can suck my hole now."

He disappears, slamming the door behind him.

The guys shift uncomfortably. Who quits football, right? Maybe it's a little scary to them. When someone leaves, it feels like they're rejecting you, even if that's not what's going on.

"Don't mind him," Rodriguez says.

"No," I say. "He's right. You guys did a lot for me."

"That's the game," Cheesy says. "That's how it works."

"Coach and I had a heart-to-heart," I say. "He told me I'm making the biggest mistake of my life."

"Coach is messed up over this," Rodriguez says. "He's been eating pork lo mein by the truckful."

"Seriously. We're gonna have to get the guy a friggin' Weight Watchers membership," Cheesy says.

"Is he right?" Rodriguez says. "Is it a mistake?"

I shrug. It's one of those answers I might not know for a long time.

Just then O. comes around the corner whistling. He sees me and the whistle dies.

"Okay," Rodriguez says. "I'd better see your ass at some games, huh?" We bump elbows, then he signals the guys, and they head into the locker room.

"Football players only," O. says. He walks past me like he's going straight into the locker room.

"I came to say thanks."

O. pauses. "For what?"

"For everything."

"I thought I set you up and ruined your life."

"Not true," I say. "I was being dramatic. And I was pissed at you. For a pretty good reason, I think."

O. blows out a breath. "I'm not proud of what I did," he says. "But I'm proud of the things we did together."

"Yeah," I say. "Anyway, I forgive you."

"Screw you, dude." O. clenches his fists. I think maybe we're going to get into it, but he stops himself.

"You know what? I forgive you, too," he says.

"Forgive me for what?"

"For using me to get famous."

"Am I famous now?" I say.

"Pretty famous."

"That doesn't suck."

"No, it most certainly does not," O. says.

There are catcalls inside the locker room. Guys horsing around. The team vibe. I miss it. At least that part of it.

A tiny part of me feels like I am making a mistake.

"I got to motivate," O. says.

"So what now?" I say. "Do you think you can be friends with someone who's not a football player?"

O. opens the locker-room door. "You don't know me well enough to know the answer to that?"

He's right. I already know.

"It was a good game," he says. "But it's over. Now I have to get ready for the next one."

He nods once, and then he goes inside to join the guys.

buses come and they go.

"Andy! Wait up a second," April says.

I'm on my way out of school, and I think about ignoring her, rushing out the door so fast she can't catch me. The thing is, I see her in AP. I see her in Gym. It's not like I can avoid her forever. So I stop.

"What's up," I say.

"You know," she says. "Lots of things."

We walk out together. I don't think we've ever walked out the front of the school together. It's a new experience for us.

"We didn't get to talk after the game," April says.

"You heard that I quit?"

"Everyone's talking about it."

"What are they saying?"

"They're angry," she says. "But I think it's because they miss you."

They. Not *I*. Big difference, right?

"I think I'm going to write for the lit journal," I say. "Try something new and different."

School buses fill up and rumble away in clouds of black smoke. I haven't been out here at this time in a couple months. It's funny how you can go away and come back, and things are just the same.

"How do you like being a cheerleader?" I say.

"It's okay," she says. "I mean, I think I'm pretty good at it."

"I think so, too."

"The truth is it's not really my thing, you know?"

"So why do you do it?" I say.

"Why did you play football?"

"I quit football."

"But why did you play in the first place?"

"There were things that I wanted from it," I say.

I look in her eyes. Soft blue, even softer than when I first met her. Maybe she's changed her contacts.

"Those things you wanted," she says. "You don't want them anymore?"

"I want different things," I say.

April looks off into the distance. She shivers and pulls her sweater around her.

"You could quit, too," I say. "Drop the cheerleading. Get back to something—I don't know—more your style."

"I'm different than you, Andy. I actually like being popular."

"I didn't exactly hate it," I say.

She laughs. "Anyway," she says, "I can't quit. The girls need me."

"For what?"

"I help them with their homework."

"I knew you helped Lisa, but—"

"All of them," she says. "We have a study group together. How do you think I got into that clique in the first place? Half of them would be going to state schools without me. So it's pretty much guaranteed they'll keep me around."

"Wow. Isn't that . . . I mean, isn't it—?"

"Kind of creepy? Definitely. But it doesn't really matter now. Once you're in, you can make changes. Influence things. Maybe bring someone into the group that you actually like. You know what I mean?"

"It's an interesting idea."

"You can't do that from the outside," April says. "From outside you're behind the window looking in. What can you do from out there but tap on the glass?"

Another bus rumbles away. I look at April, the sun hitting her from the side and lighting up her hair. She's still beautiful and smart and has great teeth, but there's something different about her now.

No, it's not her.

It's me. I see her differently. Everything in her life is a chess move, and I don't like it.

"I have to get to cheer practice," she says. "See you around?"

She says it like it's a question, like she's expecting me to make a move. Or at least try to.

The old me would have gotten really excited about that.

I say, "Take care, April."

And I get on a bus.

i see yee.

I'm sitting alone in the cafeteria.

Eytan has some UN thing to do during lunch today, so I'm not hanging out with him until later. There are a lot of people who don't want me at their table now that I'm not a football player. Some people are calling me a quitter, saying I abandoned the school. Other people don't care so much, or they missed the whole thing entirely.

There are a few places I could sit if I wanted to, but I don't feel like it. When you sit with people in high school, it's like you're declaring your allegiance. Kind of like registering to vote for a particular party. I'm not ready to be with any party. I want to be independent for a while.

Hip-hop music is booming through the cafeteria. A few hundred students signed a petition last week, and Caroline Whitney-Smith agreed to pipe in the school radio station while we eat. It's better than people sneaking in iPod speakers and having music turf wars.

Nancy Yee walks by with a tray in her hands. She doesn't look at me.

I don't know why, but I say, "Do you want to sit, Nancy?"

"Why? So you can insult me again?"

"So we can talk a little."

She bites her lip like she's having trouble making up her mind.

"Just be warned," I say. "I'm kind of radioactive right now."

"What does that have to do with me?"

"Guilt by association."

"I don't believe in that," she says.

"The rest of the school does," I say.

"That's their problem."

That does it. She sits down and arranges her tray. Salad and french fries, with nine packets of mustard stacked along the side. I look at her like she's crazy.

"That's a crime in some countries," I say.

"I love condiments. So kill me," she says, and she rips open a packet with her teeth and squeezes mustard all over the fries and salad. "You want a taste?"

"I try not to trigger my gag reflex in public."

She laughs and pushes her hair back from her face with two fingers. Her acne is still there, but it's so faint now, she just looks like she's blushing.

"Your face looks pretty good," I say.

I'm not sure if you're supposed to say things like that to a girl. Probably not.

"Thanks," she says. "My mom took me to the dermatologist. The doctor said my hair was making my face break out. I don't get how my hair and my face can't work together. I mean, they're both on the same body, right? They're even right next to each other. You'd think they'd get along better."

"I get what you mean," I say. "I wonder why I feel hungry if it's only going to make me gain weight. I'm already fat, right? So why would my body make me hungry if it will only make the situation worse?"

"I know, right?" she says. "I think our bodies do whatever they want. They kind of have their own agenda, and we don't get a vote."

I forgot that Nancy is kind of a genius. I always think of her as this scrawny, weird girl with acne, but she's not. Or she is, but she's a lot more, too.

"You hate me because I don't shop at the Gap," she says.

"It's not hate," I say. "More like shock and awe."

I notice that Nancy has pretty eyes. Dark black and very bright. Naturally dark.

"Anyway, I was being a jerk," I say.

"I agree," she says. "But if you want to shop at the mall, that's your prerogative."

"I'd love to shop at the mall. But nothing fits me there."

"Oh," she says. She rearranges the fries on her plate so they spell her name. *N-A-N-C* . . .

"I'll try one of those if you're still offering."

"Okay, but if you're going to puke, face towards the jock table."

Nancy slides her plate to me, and I eat the *N*. French fries with mustard. Kind of like a salted pretzel. Nancy may be on to something.

"I have this theory," she says. "Do you want to hear it?"

"Sure."

"Okay, everyone in school fantasizes about having a different life, right? They daydream about who they want to be and the things they're going to do when they get there. But nobody does anything about it. And when you look at adults, how many of them actually went and lived their dreams?"

Nancy stabs a french fry, then a chunk of salad, then another french fry. I watch it turn to yellow mush in her mouth.

"So what's the theory?" I say.

"Dreams have gravity. You think a dream is pushing you forward, but it's actually sucking you back towards it. That's why people get stuck. That's my theory, at least."

"So we should all stop dreaming?"

"No. We should do something about it. Take action. Like you," she says.

"What did I do?"

"You broke through the gravitational field. You played football."

"I never thought of it like that."

"How did you think of it?"

"I thought I was a sellout," I say.

"No way. You're kind of like an astronaut."

"When you put it like that, I sound pretty cool."

"Speaking of gag reflexes," she says, and clears her throat.

That makes me laugh. Suddenly I get a strange feeling in my chest, and I start to sweat under my arms.

"Do you want to get a pizza bagel after school?" I say. "You can put mustard on it."

Nancy looks at me, surprised. I'm pretty surprised, too.

"You mean like a date?" she says.

"Kind of like that," I say.

The fourth-period bell rings. Kids groan all around the cafeteria. Nancy doesn't move.

"Can I ask you a serious question?" she says.

I nod.

"Did you notice me back then?"

"When?" I say.

"You know. Last year. The beginning of school. Whenever."

"Honestly?"

"Yeah."

"You were kind of invisible to me."

She bites down hard. I think she's going to tell me she doesn't want to go on a date, but she just nods her head slowly.

"I didn't think so," she says.

"But I see you now," I say.

We look into each other's eyes, and I feel that feeling again. It's a little tough to breathe. Not like when I'm having an asthma attack, but something different.

A second bell rings. That's the warning bell. Caroline Whitney-Smith loves a good warning bell.

"That pizza-bagel thing sounds good," Nancy says. "I'll see you after school, okay?"

"Great," I say.

We both stand up, and Nancy grabs her sketchbook. The music stops playing in the background. I don't hear the song anymore, but I can still hear the beat.

Thump. Thump. Thump.

At least I think it's the beat. It could be my heart. It's going pretty hard right now. Hearts do that sometimes, all on their own, and they don't even bother to ask your permission.

acknowledgments

To my high-school posse from so long ago: Josh, Darrin, Ethan, Peter, Jon, Paul, and our other friends from Brighton High School in Rochester, New York. Though the story is fictional, the feelings are not. Thank you for the inspiration.

I'm so grateful to Stuart Krichevsky, Kathryne Wick, and Shana Cohen at SK. Your support and encouragement means the world to me.

Much thanks to Doug Pocock and Elizabeth Law, who brought me in and gave my work a home. Thanks, too, to the great team at Egmont. You really know how to make an author feel welcome.

Thanks to Lucy Stille and Zadoc Angell at Paradigm for taking things to the next level.

Thanks to Aaron Lee, Adam Silberstein, and Doug Hill, amazing men who point the way every day.

Thanks to the sweet and brilliant Kauser for keeping me sane after the fact.

Finally, a very special thanks to Stephanie Hubbard, writer and friend, who helped me so much while I was creating this book.

To read a sample chapter from
Allen Zadoff's next book

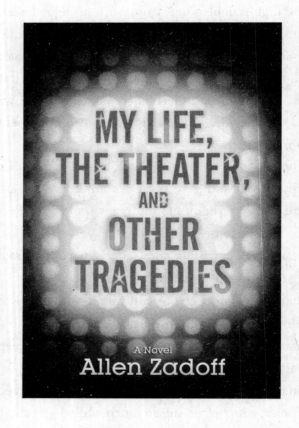

please visit
www.egmontusa.com/sneakpeeks